Whiskey Woman

Written By: Kelly Jarrell

To Jane,

Have enjoyed service
with you in team ministry
doing Christ's
work.

Jim

COPYRIGHT PAGE

Copyright © 2016 **Kelly Jarrell**

All rights reserved. No part of this publication may be reproduced, distributed, or transmitted in any form or by any means, including photocopying, recording, or other electronic or mechanical methods, without the prior written permission of the publisher, except in the case of brief quotations embodied in critical reviews and certain other non-commercial uses permitted by copyright law.

Acknowledgements

I would like to thank God for giving me the ability to use my talents to write. I want to thank my Mama, Patty Davis, for helping me after the death of my husband. I'm thankful to my daughter's, Ashley and Jessica, my sister's, Tammy King, and Kim Cordle, my friends, Sabrina Scott, and Margaret Rice, for reading my books and believing in me. For my facebook friends, Carol Johnson, for editing and formatting my books at no charge to me, just because she loves me, Jason Deckard, for always having my back, Karen and Carsten Sommer-you two are the role model for the perfect marriage, and to Sabrina and Roy Hackworth-I want one too...lol. (inside joke). Thanks to my therapist, Denise Burgy for keeping me sane (well, mostly anyway), and thanks to my friends, Zane, Rhonda, and Ron for taking time out of your lives to cheer me up. A special thanks to my friend, Johnathon Bystra, for always making me laugh. I love you all. Last, but not least, I want to thank my pastor's wife, Ann, for being a loyal reader and friend. Biggest thanks to all those who buy my books and show such loving support. You're the reason I keep writing. I hope you enjoy reading Whiskey Woman as much as I did writing it.

Table of Contents

Acknowledgements v
Chapter One 1
Chapter Two 5
Chapter Four 8
Chapter Five 10
Chapter Six 15
Chapter Seven 18
Chapter Eight 21
Chapter Nine 25
Chapter Ten 27
Chapter Eleven 36
Chapter Twelve 43
Chapter Thirteen 48
Chapter Fourteen 50
Chapter Fifteen 54
Chapter Sixteen 59
Chapter Seventeen 62
Chapter Eighteen 67
Chapter Nineteen 71
Chapter Twenty 73
Chapter Twenty-One 76
Chapter Twenty-Two 80
Chapter Twenty-Three 82
Chapter Twenty-Four 86
Chapter Twenty-Five 90

Chapter Twenty-Six 95

Chapter Twenty-Seven 99

Chapter Twenty-Six 102

Chapter Twenty-Seven 104

Chapter Twenty-Eight 111

Chapter Twenty-Nine 116

Chapter Thirty 121

Chapter Thirty-One 128

Chapter Thirty-Two 132

About The Author 137

Chapter One

Prestonsburg, Ky. 2003

Tempest Hawthorne faced the three God's of Eternity-God of Love, God of Life, and the God of Judgment. Her fate now lay in their hands alone, after she lost her battle with death. She had been murdered by her own husband. Although she didn't feel the sting of death, she was pretty bummed out to find herself in front of a council of Gods in the afterlife. She had no clue about what was happening right now. All three were sitting upon thrones made of gold and ivory. She had always thought that when a person dies, they go to Heaven, or Hell, but she was wrong. Since her arrival here, she had been guided by an Angel named Destiny. Destiny was beautiful. She had a round face, that held her perfectly bowed mouth, and flowery-blue eyes, with curly locks of honey-blonde hair framing her angelic face, and Tempest judged her to be around her mid-forties. She had an eternal glow about her that did not come from a light bulb. She floated beside Tempest as they made their way down the golden path to the room of Thrones. Destiny had explained what would happen once she arrived there, but Tempest only half-listened, because she was taking in way too much stimulus.

There were no highways here. Just roads paved with gold and silver. Tempest didn't know why they had roads, since the Angels floated around. None of them appeared to even have any feet. That was strange. Also, everywhere that grass should've been, there were wildflowers instead. It was beautiful, but not very functional, or so Tempest thought any way. She briefly wondered what the animals would eat, but she need not worry long. Each animal had their own yard here, and it was the only place where grass was planted, and flourished. Destiny explained that the grass and flowers never died here, or faded. Tempest could see family members gathered together in each house there. All the babies had gossamer wings, and they flew around giggling and gurgling happily it seemed. Tempest wondered if any of her relatives were here somewhere, waiting for her arrival.

"Destiny. Is this Heaven?"

"Yes Tempest, this is Heaven."

"Are any of my family members here?"

Destiny hesitated. "You do have family members here, but you can't see them just yet."

"Why not?" Tempest beseeched her.

Destiny frowned. "You must face the council first."

"The *council*...?"

"Yes Tempest, the Council. You must go there first, so they can decide what to do with you."

"I'm dead. What's to figure out?" she huffed.

"They have to decide together if you're going to stay in Heaven, go to Hell, or return back to Earth and do a job before entering Heaven for eternity."

"You have got to be kidding me! I was just shot to death by my husband! I am just thirty-one years old! It's true I didn't attend Church regularly, but I am a good person-I swear I am!" Tempest was clearly upset now. She couldn't believe she was dead already. She still couldn't wrap her mind around the fact that her own husband had murdered her! *Steve I hope you rot in Hell you bastard!!*

"Tsk tsk." Destiny chastened her. "You're supposed to have only pure thoughts Tempest. You're about to meet the Council."

As if on cue, Tempest noticed a double door in front of them. It hadn't been there before. She didn't dare open it. She was scared now. She glanced at the doors and saw her image staring back at her. The mirrors were clearer than mirrors she'd stood in front of on earth. She gasped at her image. She didn't look like any kind of angel she could think of. Instead, she looked like death. A portion of the left side of her brain had been shot off, blood splattered her clothing, and her coloring was grayish-yellowish. "My God! I hope they can give me a new face! I look absolutely horrid!" she exclaimed aloud.

It was probably the first and only time an angel rolled her eyes, and Tempest noticed. "*What*??"

Destiny just shook her head in frustration. "Never mind...just go in already. I'll be waiting right here for you, and Tempest? Try not to swear in front of them. They are Gods you know..."

Tempest opened one of the doors, and muttered, "Oh God..."

Destiny crossed her fingers. This one was definitely going to cause some trouble-she just knew it!

Comanche Camp 1865

Gentle Soul watched his rival fall under his arrow, and turned to aim at another Comanchero bent on killing, raping, or maiming his Cheyenne people. He had not wanted to go to war with anyone, but the Comancheros had come looking for it. After killing another one, Gentle Soul caught movement out of the corner of his eye. There, only twenty foot from where he fought, was a band of them gathered in a circle at his tepee. Gentle Soul felt his heart quiver in dread. His wife, Silent Speaks, was the main focus in the group gathered, and he could only imagine what was taking place, as he fought his way closer to the group who surrounded her while they raped her and even stabbed her belly-killing the child she carried.

In the space of mere minutes, Gentle Soul broke free from his attackers long enough to reach the crowd. What he saw made his blood boil. Silent Speaks was on the ground, with her dress up over her shoulders and her head at an unusual angle. He could see death in her opened eyes, and fear. It was clear that her neck had been broken and she had been raped by the men around her. He broke through the men and bent down to close her eyes. There were four of them. Two roughly grabbed him and held him down, while two more beat him nearly to death, and left him lying beside the dead body of the woman he had loved for three summers. He vowed to kill every last one of them if he survived.

Chapter Two

Tempest walked through the door and stepped on to the red carpet that led up to the three thrones. She could feel their steady gaze upon her, so she took her time, not sure at all what to think of this. Just twelve hours ago, she was telling her husband, Steve good night, and making her way up their winding staircase to their bedroom. Five hours after that, she had opened her eyes to find him standing over her, with a 9mm held to her right temple, asking her to forgive him for what he was about to do. She never got the chance to answer the bastard. She thought it was rather odd that when she was on the gurney in the emergency room, she felt herself leave her body, and she lingered above herself- hovering like an angel. But she wasn't an angel. Angels didn't walk around with their heads bloodied. She would have to ask these Gods about that, because she couldn't very well walk around here disfigured, could she?

"Tempest Hawthorne, we have gathered together to decide what happens to you next. Do you have anything you'd like to say to us, while we consider what happens next?" The one speaking was the God of life.

Tempest cleared her throat and answered, "Well sure I do, I don't think it was fair to let me be killed off by my rat bastar-um, my husband. So, can we kill him instead?"

The God of Judgment spoke now. "Is that what you truly want to ask us, now that you're standing here before us, Tempest?"

Tempest nodded, but kept talking. "...well that, and whether or not y'all will fix my head. It looks horrible! How am I supposed to represent heaven if I look like hell? And hey-can you set me up to float around too? I'd like to keep my feet though. Also, if for some reason, you and the gang send me back; can I NOT be married this time to Steve?"

The God of Love questioned her. "What kind of man would you like, if we were to send you back?"

Tempest jumped all over his question. "I just want a good man. You know-a man that would rather protect me, than hurt me, a strong man...a man with strong morals would be nice...let's see...and tall, dark, and handsome would work."

"Is that all?" He asked her.

"Well, as long as I'm asking...he doesn't have to be rich, but if he could be the chief instead of just another Indian, that would help, cause I'm tired of working myself to death for a man who could care less for me, ya' know?" When she got no answer back, she continued talking. "It would be nice to have a man with old values...he should be spiritual I think, but most of all, I just want a man with a good heart. One that can love me as I am-well, minus the whole head bashed in thingy..."

"Enough." The God of life spoke up. "Leave us to decide your fate." He said ominously.

Chapter three-1867

She was amused. Tempest found herself lying in a corn field in God only knew where! She raised herself up, and her hands went to her head. She was shocked-but delighted! Her head was not bashed in anymore! She looked down the length of her entire body. She wasn't in her bloody clothes any longer. Instead, she wore a gown of white, with the sleeves and hem stitched in gold. She lifted the gown to discover her feet. She smiled. Her feet were enclosed in flat gold sandals too. She noticed the diamond encrusted gold belt that fit securely around her tiny waist. Not exactly what she would've chosen to wear, but at least it wasn't bloody. Now, if she only knew what part of town she was in...She got to her feet and looked in all four directions. Her surroundings didn't reveal much. She saw a tree line to the left of the corn field, and that was all she saw, besides the corn stalks, so she decided to follow it. It shouldn't take long for a car to find her walking. She was glad the Council had decided not to send her to hell. She thought Heaven was pretty, but she wasn't ready for that either. Nope-she was however, ready to get back to her life, and hopefully, she'd see Steve very soon. She smiled at the image. This day was going to be just wonderful, she thought to herself as she began walking...

Gentle Soul walked the tree line while leaving the graves of his wife, and other family members. Since the attack on his village, that took so many lives, he had become Chief over his tribe. Silent Speaks would have been proud of him, he knew. Both of his parents had died long before the ambush on his village. His only brother, Fox Tail, who had been the chief since his Father's passing, had died in the ambush as well. Gentle Soul missed them all today and thought of every one whom he had loved and lost. Today he felt the winds stir against his mahogany skin. His black hair rustled in the wind, and touched his face gently. His big black eyes held a lot of history in them. They had seen more than their share of suffering and death. Gentle Soul's heart was heavy with sorrow over the loss of so many loved ones. He knelt down and lifted his voice in prayer.

"Spirit God, please help me on the remainder of my journey here. Look after my loved ones, and bless the streams with many trout to eat, and much Buffalo and deer upon the land to kill for meat and clothing. I let Silent Speaks go fully to you today, as I have grieved many moons, and now it is time to move on. If you bless me with another woman, please make her strong as any warrior, so that she will not die by the white man's hands like Silent Speaks did. Let her be bold, unafraid of men, and full of fire in her eyes. I pray she be easy to look upon, and be hard to tame in joining herself to all men who would try to bed her. This I ask to ensure she not be weak, where the enemy could break her. Let me be the only man who tames her wild spirit."

Chapter Four

Tempest had to laugh. After following the tree line for nearly forty minutes, she finally found someone who might help. She wondered if the Village People were in town for a show. If so, they were missing the Indian, cause he was walking towards her right now. She was excited! She hadn't ever met anyone famous before. Besides, she was tired of walking, and she hadn't spotted one damn vehicle yet. She would beg the Indian to give her a ride, if she had to.

Gentle Soul was surprised to discover a white eyes out here all by herself-and upset. Didn't the woman know what danger awaited her in these desolate hills? He was on guard instantly, for an ambush. He would have to handle this one with care. He advanced on her quickly, and gave his most fierce war cry. The little fool jumped up and down excitedly, and he knit his brows together, not at all sure he believed what he was seeing. *Was the white woman mad in the head? Where was her husband? Was he dead?* She must be delusional, he thought to himself. Yes-that had to be it. No white woman in her right mind would be out here in this unforgiving land all by herself, and running towards him. He stood still and waited on her.

Tempest was breathing hard. She really needed to start doing Pilates again. When she reached Gentle Soul, she put her hand on his muscled arm, and bent over to cough. "So sorry-I think I'm going to cough up a lung…"

This bit of news scared Gentle Soul. "Tell me how I can help you keep your lung."

Tempest laughed. "Wow-you're good at this Indian-thing!" she said, as she rose up from her coughing spell. "Where's the rest of the band?"

Gentle Soul looked confused. "I am by myself. There is no band with me today."

"Okay, we can play this thing as long as you want, but I need to get home. Can you be a dear and let me use your cell phone?" she held her hand out expectantly, but he never gave her one.

Tempest was getting a little frustrated. "Let me guess, you didn't bring it with you, did you?"

"I know not what you speak of white woman."

"Are you drunk this early in the day?"

"No. Are you?" he countered.

Tempest glared openly at Gentle Soul. "Where's your vehicle Kumo-sabi?"

"My name is Gentle Soul. I don't know what the vehicle is you're talking about."

Tempest did an eyes roll-twice. "It's how we get around. Remember? It goes vroom, vroom...?" She mimicked her hands moving on an invisible steering wheel for him.

"You must be feverish." Gentle Soul held his hand out to her. "Come with me white woman. I will take you to my village and see that medicine woman works her magic on you."

Chapter Five

"I'm sorry, but medicine woman's going to have to wait for now, big guy. I have to get home, take a shower, and get revenge on my husband for killing me. So, if you don't mind, just please tell me where the road is please, and I'll be on my way."

Gentle Soul ran a hand over his disbelieving face. The woman wasn't right in the head-this much he was sure of, but what could he do with her? She needed help. He would have to take her back to his village-no two ways about it.

Tempest went very still as she felt his eyes moving over her. He was watching her close, and she wondered what it was that he was thinking now. She studied him as well, taking in his tall, muscular figure. Although she was tall for a woman, he was a good four inches taller than her 5'8". His chest was bare, and showed off his very impressive body. His arms were well muscled-as was the rest of his body that she could see. He wore buckskins to enclose his legs. His jet black hair whipped around his face, and she zeroed in on his mouth. Looking at his beauty gave her butterflies in her stomach.

"You come with me, to my village."

Tempest bristled at his command. "I'm not going anywhere with you. I don't even know you Mister! Besides, I have to get home now. I have a lot of business to take care of."

Gentle Soul was perplexed at her. "White woman, please close your mouth for once."

"Look Indian-wanna-be-The gig is up, okay? I don't know what you're trying to accomplish by playing like an Indian, but I'm not into role-playing. If you're not going to help me, then get out of my way while I walk past you, because I have to get back home! Okay?" she huffed, with both hands on her hips.

"You say too many words that make no sense. Come now..." he said, offering her his hand once more.

"Oh brother! No!" she turned back in the direction she had come from, and started walking away from the crazy-ass, when she felt two strong arms entrap her, twirl her around to face him, then yelped when he went low and grabbed both legs from behind, then tossed her effortlessly over his shoulder. Tempest was raging mad now. She squirmed, and kicked to no avail. "You piece of dog shit-let me down!"

"Gentle Soul will let you down when we reach my village. You're very sick, heh? Medicine woman will help you regain your mind. The harder you fight, the more difficult it will be for you."

Tempest snorted her disgust. "This is kidnapping you sorry son-of-a-bitch! Let me down, or I swear I'll hurt you, and get your hands off my ass pervert!"

"My name is Gentle Soul, and I'm sorry if you're uncomfortable, but you need strong medicine. You talk out of your head white woman."

"Listen up Gentle Soul, I have a name too-it's Tempest. Tempest Hawthorne. I'm not talking crazy either. You're the one acting like an Indian for God's sake!" she spat at him.

"This is not an act Tempest. I am an Indian. You should be relieved that I found you when I did, or you may have been taken by comencheros, or hostile Indians."

"So I should thank you then, for kidnapping me? Well, thank you so damn much Gentle Soul. I promise you, when I get near a phone; you're going to have the cops breaking down your door for forcing me to go with you; and I will rat you out...you'll see. I'll be your worst nightmare Gentle Soul!"

Gentle Soul stopped and bent down to release Tempest. "Gentle Soul thinks you're already too much trouble, but cannot leave you here alone or you'd see an early death."

Whiskey Woman

Tempest would've fallen had he not caught her in his arms, and she couldn't very well push him away, since she had needles running through her legs. He had her caught up almost flush against him, and for the first time, Tempest really noticed him. His piercing eyes were black as coal, and penetrated to her very core, as a woman. She knew that this moment would stay with her-him holding her against him, while she drank in the sight of him. He really did look like a real Indian. Whoever had done his makeup was spot on! In fact, he looked natural in it. And the outfit was indecent, but she had to admit, it fit in all the right places on his body. She had no doubt that if he were truly an Indian he'd make every squaw want to claim him as their warrior, and it unsettled her to even think about it. *Get a grip girl!* "If you're an Indian, why do you speak perfect English?"

"My Father met a missionary years ago who offered to teach our village English. My entire village can speak it now without too much difficulty."

Gentle Soul held Tempest against him. This close embrace gave him an opportunity to notice her eyes too. They were whiskey colored, and matched her full head of hair that had fallen loose from a circled band she wore in her hair. He thought about the two resembling each other so much, and when he looked at her again, he knew there was something strangely beautiful about her-with eyes and hair that same color, it made him think of fire. He wondered where her man was-and why he had tried to kill her. Was she even telling him the truth? He feared she suffered greatly from a high fever. Before he could think, he pressed his lips to her forehead, and she was cool to the touch. *How was that possible? The white woman had been speaking nonsense ever since he met her. She had to be sick!* He pulled back and took her shoulders in his hands to look at all of her again. She was clothed like a Chief's bride, he noticed. He wondered how talented she was to have made stitches that were not seen by the eye up close. Confused, he let go of her, and pushed away from her.

"If you promise not to run from me, I will let you walk beside me until we reach the river ahead. There we will mount my horse and ride until the sun sets. Tomorrow, we will ride into my village where you will be safe, and looked after." He offered her.

Whiskey Woman

Tempest was getting tired of the whole act already. "Let me guess. You're going to take me to your village where I will be forced to see a medicine woman so she can give me cloves or vitamins to eat for my craziness, and then I'll be alright, but in the meantime, I'm going to fall in love with you, right?"

Before he could answer, she started again, "Let me guess again- you're dad is the Chief of this place. Am I right Gentle Soul?" she quipped.

"He used to be. I am the Chief of my people now. How did you know about my father? Do you practice magic?"

"I try to limit myself to one magic trick a day. Just call me special and shit."

"No. I will call you Whiskey. It fits you perfectly."

Tempest bristled. "Enough already! Can we cut the act and talk like normal people do? I want to go home. Please! Can't you take me home Gentle Soul? I'm very tired. I have had one helluva' day..."

"I have to do what is best for you. You talk out of your head. I cannot let you go until medicine woman helps you. It is the way of my people."

Tempest raised her voice to him. "Listen up Gentle Soul. I'm not asking you-I'm telling you! I can find town on my own. You can go back to the village people, and nobody has to know this happened. I swear I won't tell another living person, but you have to let me go now, okay?" she looked at him for a sign he would let her go finally, but he was stubborn as a jack ass!

"Enough talk! You can go with me willingly, or I can carry you; it's your choice Whiskey Woman." She could see the set of his jaw and knew he meant it. Like it or not-she was going to see the village people! Without answering, she started briskly walking, since her anger gave her fresh adrenaline. He would pay for doing this, she told herself, and she couldn't wait to see it either.

An hour later, they had finally reached his horse-a black stallion no less. "Pfft! Couldn't you be more imaginative? The black stallion is so overused, don't ya' think?" she grumbled, but after he got atop the horse, she didn't refuse when he held his hand out for her. "Just so ya' know, I'm give out, or I woulda' fought you on this horse. I'm scared of horses, but too tired to argue."

Gentle Soul smiled for once. *My God! He was more like a Greek God when he flashed those pearly whites at her. She would have to keep her mind on getting away from him, not running into his arms every time he smiled. He really should quit that already...*

Chapter Six

Gentle Soul knew the moment Whiskey woman fell asleep. She had held her back straight for two hours, and he knew she must be tired from the strain of it. It couldn't be helped. He would have to let her realize that on her own, and she did. She slumped against him, and he tightened his arms around her naturally, although being with her was nowhere near natural. Now that she was asleep, he could think. It was hard to concentrate when she was awake. She had lots of spirit- Too much if you asked him. He preferred his women to be sweet-natured. This woman was nowhere near sweet. She had a barbed tongue and used it frequently. If she were a warrior, he would've been proud of her fire, but as a woman, it irritated him to no end. Her head bobbed forward, and he pulled her back more securely, fitting her head just under his chin; and she fell into a deeper sleep after awhile. He would have to make camp soon. His horse, Black Wing, could not go much longer without food and rest. Black Wing was now with foal in her belly. Soon, she would give him a baby. He was glad. He loved Black Wing. He had received Black Wing from his father, it was the last thing hls father had ever given him, and he had spent two summers breaking him, and teaching him useful tricks. Silent Speaks had been afraid of Black Wing. He supposed because the horse was many hands taller than most. He knew Silent Speaks couldn't control such a high-spirited horse, so he never asked her to ride him. Instead, she rode a more tame horse when they traveled. The Indians that had killed his wife had also killed her horse, so he buried them side by side. He felt his mood begin to darken, so he focused on the hills that were now harder to see in the darkness descending. He knew he had better make camp now, so he looked for a good spot, before waking Tempest up.

Tempest awoke with a start when Gentle Soul stopped Black Wing. "Hold on to the mane." He instructed her. She held on with both hands while he dismounted, then turned to grab her down from the horse too.

Tempest slid down his hard body and shivered, but not from the cold. As soon as her feet hit the ground, she removed herself from his arms and stood away from him, as if wary of what he'd do next. She watched him silently gather twigs to start a fire, and then he gathered enough pine braches to make a bedding area big enough for both of them. *Them? Oh hell no!!!*

"I'm not sleeping with you, if that's what you're thinking. Hell, I barely even know you. I didn't even sleep with Steve, and he was my husband for Christ's sake!" Gentle Soul took out a pouch from around his waist and produced a very sharp knife. Tempest swallowed hard and backed away-slowly. "Umm, listen, if you hurt me, people will come looking for you-bad people!" she stammered aloud.

Gentle Soul almost laughed at Tempest. It was obvious she thought he meant to use the knife on her. "Be still Whiskey. I must hunt for our belly's to be full tonight." He could see the thought of him hunting made her hopeful. "Don't think about walking away from camp. The coyotes would eat you alive. Besides, I won't be too far from you. And, if you're thinking of running off, I must warn you that either commencheros or rogue Indians would love to have a white woman as their company, before raping you; then eventually killing you."

His words shook her more than she let on, but she would get away from him, even if it did kill her. "What am I supposed to do while you go kill Bambi?" Gentle Soul never responded; as he walked away, missing her stomp both of her feet. Tempest was tired of being ordered around by a man who thought she was crazy, even though he was the one with delusions. *Go figure cupcake!*

Gentle Soul had been gone for a good half an hour before Tempest decided she should go ahead and run now, while she had the chance. She knew if he was close he'd just stop her. She was hungry, and on foot. She didn't know if she'd make it to town or not, but she had to try damn it! She pulled back her shoulders and headed away from the fire, and Gentle Soul. She had only walked five hundred feet or so when she heard horses, and plenty of them, at the sound of it...

Whiskey Woman

When the three riders came upon her, she felt her heart plummet in fear. She counted nine of them. All nine of the men were dirty and they openly leered at her. None of them were white or Indian. This must be the Comancheros Gentle Soul told her about. She could feel goose bumps all over her body, and shivered. She easily picked out their leader. He was in front, and barked orders while seeing right through her. The other two men jumped down from their horses and grabbed her. "Oh hell nooo! Not again..." she spat in disbelief...

Chapter Seven

Gentle Soul heard the horses and ran back to camp for Tempest, but she was gone. *Damn stubborn woman!* He dropped the rabbit he held and followed their voices. He should've never left the little fool alone. If they made it out of here alive, he sure as hell wouldn't make the same mistake twice.

There were too many of them to fight by himself. He hid just out of sight and watched them; waiting for any mistake that might help him save Tempest. Four of them held her-they had to, because she was being quite the hell-cat. He wondered if she ever shut that pretty mouth of hers.

Tempest raked her nails down the face of one of them, and she was glad to see twin paths of blood on his face; but he was livid with anger.

"You bitch!" he exclaimed, and then struck her face as hard as he could, making her teeth clench in pain and shock. *They really are like wild animals...Please help me, she thought to herself.* Her mouth hurt where he had busted her lip, but it didn't stop her from telling him exactly what she thought of him.

"Don't you dare lay your filthy hands on me again, you bunch of swine! I mean it, you'll regret it!" They all three laughed at her openly.

The leader spoke first. "You won't be so wicked with that tongue once I've mounted you." He warned her.

She spat at him. "I wouldn't try that if I were you. I've already been kidnapped once today, and I'm getting pretty damned mad right about now." When they all laughed at her, it only fueled her anger. "I'm glad you think kidnapping and rape are funny, because where you're going, you'll need a sense of humor when you all become someone else's bitch!"

One of the two men spoke up. "And where will we be going?"

"To start with, you'll go to prison, but then you'll die and have to answer to the three Gods, like I did. I'm sure you'll all be sent to hell, so don't worry-you'll all be right at home together."

Their leader sneered at her. He was not amused any longer. "Tie her hands and lay her face up on the ground." He instructed his men.

Once she was tied and on the ground, one of the men stuffed her mouth with a dirty rag. She gagged.

"No. Take the gag out. I want to hear her scream beneath me when I break her in just right." He jeered.

Once her mouth was free again, she let him have it! "I wouldn't look so smug if I were you, dumb ass. "

"Oh really? And please tell me why you wouldn't."

"Because there's an Indian right behind you, and he looks angry to me."

He laughed. "You really are crazy, aren't you?" He began to unbutton his pants in front of her. Crazy or not-she was a fiery woman who needed to have her spirit broken, and he was just the man to do it. He ordered the other five to look for dry branches to start a fire. He wanted to be alone with her, to teach her a lesson she'd never forget. Nobody smarted off to him like she had, but he would make sure she didn't again.

Gentle Soul caught two of them by surprise. He plunged his knife into the first one, and then broke the second man's neck quickly. He would have to kill the other three in front of him if he was to get away with Tempest before the others came back. He was proud of Tempest for fighting them. Even an Indian woman would have remained silent, and right now, he was glad she wasn't an Indian woman-no matter how crazy she might be. He moved in closer, keeping his eyes on the three left. He could see Tempest's face more clearly now, and it angered him greatly to see her mouth swollen and bleeding. Her eyes latched onto his, and he could see her fear. In an instance, he was on two of the men who held her, and all three of them fell to the ground, each man fighting for his life. That left only their leader for now, but when Gentle Soul looked up, he found him gone.

"I'm here for the white woman." Gentle Soul told the four on the ground. None of them responded back to him. "What is the name of your cowardly leader who left you all here to die?"

"Jesus Cruz."

"Enough words." Gentle Soul delivered another bone-jarring blow to the man's head that spoke to him. "Tell Cruz to stay away from the white woman. She is under my strong arm now, and I will defend her to the death…"

Gentle Soul came to her then and produced his knife to cut her bindings. Tempest was never so happy to see him as she was now. "Run back to camp Whiskey."

"No. I'm not leaving you Gentle Soul."

Gentle Soul considered her words. "Now you know what happens when you try to. Go. I will follow after I bury the bodies." He commanded her.

"But they're nor even dead…" She stated, and Gentle Soul only smiled a cruel smile.

"…yet…now go!"

Tempest didn't need to be told again. She turned around and ran as fast as her legs would take her back into their camp, and waited-on him to join her. She wondered if Gentle Soul was alright. She felt badly about causing him any trouble, but damn it, she didn't belong here! If he would just steer her in the right direction she could be anywhere but here.

This was nonsense. The man was touched in the head for goodness sakes! Why did it matter to her if something sinister was happening? After all, it was him that had kidnapped her. The way she figured it-he deserved to be taken to task over forcing her to go with him to his "village." But secretly, she hoped he was on his way back to her, and that he would be alright. Within a few minutes, he had done just that. She was glad he did.

Chapter Eight

Gentle Soul was not happy when he got back to camp, after burying all eight men. It had been a blood bath for sure after the other four had returned, but the Gods had been with him, thankfully. He didn't recognize any of the men but one-Cruz. Cruz was their leader and it was by his command his wife had been raped and murdered. He had to fight too many of Cruz's men to try and go after Cruz himself, but Gentle Soul would find him again and kill him for what he had done to Silent Speaks. For now it was late, and he was hungry. He knew Tempest must be hungry as well, but he found her asleep by the dying fire, huddled up to keep warm. He watched the rise and fall of her chest and felt a certain protectiveness for her. He reasoned within himself that it was because she was obviously not well. He broke his stare long enough to skin the rabbit and roast it over the open fire he had built back up.

No doubt about it, the woman was quite inviting to look at. He'd have to look away from her often, because he knew she was sickly. It was a shame though-he couldn't help but like her. She had real fire in her. Looking at her now though-you'd never guess that she did. Her mouth was open slightly in her sleep, and he studied it. There was dried blood marring her perfectly shaped lips. Her lashes lay darkly against her upper cheek, and wrapped in the gold dress she wore, she reminded him of what whites called, "a present." He called her name softly, as to not frighten her.

"Whiskey..."

Tempest heard him calling her, but she needed to get warm.

"Wake up Whiskey. I have made you rabbit to fill your tummy. Sit up and eat with me."

Gentle Soul took a pouch of water from his horse and dipped his fingers in it. Again he walked over to Tempest, and knelt low enough to touch his wet fingers against her mouth. Tempest jumped into a sitting position.

"What the hell are you doing Gentle Soul?"

"I'm cleaning the blood on your mouth Whiskey, so you can eat. Aren't you hungry?"

Tempest started to tell him no, but the food smelled way too good. Instead, she asked, "What is it?"

"Rabbit."

"No chicken or steak? Cheeseburgers…?"

"No Whiskey, rabbit, just rabbit for now. I will feed you better once we get to my village."

"Oh Gentle Soul, why do you insist on claiming to be a real Indian? Do you truly believe what you tell me?"

Gentle Soul studied her eyes. Eyes were the window to the soul, he knew. She appeared to be genuinely concerned for him, but he couldn't understand why she insisted that he wasn't an Indian. "Whiskey, do you hate the Indians so much that you simply cannot accept my red skin?"

Tempest could hear the hurt in his voice, and she felt bad for what she knew must be said. "Gentle Soul, I don't know what else to say, except that I have never felt badly against Indians. I'm just worried that you're not facing reality."

Gentle Soul felt hope die in him. He had hoped she was merely scared of him as an Indian, but no, she had a very troubled mind. "No more talk Whiskey. We must get rest for the long ride tomorrow."

The sun was out the next day, and Tempest enjoyed the feel of it on her skin. After breaking camp this morning, Gentle Soul had remained quiet. She didn't like this side of him. She would rather be fighting with him than face his silence. They had ridden for almost three hours. Tempest wondered what had put him in a mood that kept him so quiet.

Whiskey Woman

It had been a long night for her. Even though Gentle Soul had kept the fire going, she had still shivered from the night chill. She was quite surprised when he made them a pallet and told her to lie down next to him. At first, she had been stiff and weary, but right before she had closed her eyes, she had nestled up to his heat. She was too tired to keep vigil last night. So she didn't even fight sleep. She did however dream that Gentle Soul had wrapped her in his arms and made sure she was safe from the Comancheros. She didn't like depending on a man for anything, but after her troubled day, she felt a lot better with him lying next to her; though she'd never tell him that.

They rode steadily, to make their way to his village before nightfall. During the day's ride, Tempest was amazed at how lovely the country side was. They still hadn't came anywhere near a road, or any people for that matter. It was strange. Everything her eyes could take in made no sense to her. The land was barren and not developed as it should've been. Tempest wondered if they were even in Kentucky. Nothing she saw seemed familiar to her.

"Gentle Soul, what part of Kentucky are we in right now?"

"We are in Oklahoma Whiskey."

"Oklahoma? Surely that can't be! I'm from Kentucky!"

Gentle Soul dropped his head. "Whiskey, nothing is as you think it is. Did you hit your head before I found you?"

Tempest gave a bitter laugh. "Not quite hit...more like got it blown off..."

"How is that possible Whiskey? I see no marks on you."

Tempest sighed. "...that's because they gave me my head and face back before coming here."

Gentle Soul put up both hands in mock surrender. "No more talking foolishness. Soon, you will be cared for, and everything will be alright."

Gentle Soul thought about the previous night, and scowled in remembrance. Tempest was too much temptation. He would not take advantage of her though. All he wanted to do was get her to his medicine woman and try to help her. He thought about her lying next to him, and sleeping. She looked like a goddess in her clothing. Her dress had hiked up to her thighs-exposing sun-kissed lean and long legs. He watched the rise and fall of each breath she took for awhile. Although her clothing concealed her breasts, he didn't miss how they held up her dress. She had been blessed with very generous breasts, and he liked them very much. Her hips flared out-giving her the perfect figure. The camp fire had sent dancing lights through her dark hair, and she was quite a beauty. He had felt his manhood begin to harden and rise, so he turned away from her and put his back against hers, as not to disturb her. Yes, it was a very long night. He knew he had to be on his best behavior though. She seemed to have gone through a lot. He didn't want to add to her troubles.

Chapter Nine

Steve Hawthorne was living large. It had been two years since his wife had died on an operating table. Two years, and still nobody knew that he had caused her death. In fact, all their friends and family felt sorry for his loss. He chuckled bitterly. It felt good to be single again. He enjoyed the insurance money, and the ladies enjoyed him taking them out to spend it. He often wondered what Tempest had been thinking when he put the gun up to her head. He was sure that no one suspected foul play, and he was glad they didn't.

Tempest was beloved by all who knew her. He'd never seen such an outpouring of love and grief before. Mourners grieved her death as if she were a princess. That bothered him to no end. Tempest had always been a thorn in his side. He was sick and tired of hearing her name on his family and friends lips, but how could he tell them to shut up? He was beginning to consider moving away from their hometown, and starting over somewhere new. After all, everything he had now was paid off thanks to the insurance money, and he had enough money to retire if he chose to do so.

He walked around the house, taking every detail in as he moved from room to room. It was like she was still here-lingering. He didn't feel any guilt though, he only felt irritated at her silent presence in his life. Killing her should have been enough, but it wasn't. Her memory haunted him daily. He could still remember seeing the look on her face-pure shock and hurt. What else could he have done? He knew it would have only been a matter of time before she divorced him. She was a published author, and on her way up in this world. He couldn't let her leave him.

Tempest had wanted children so badly she had begged him. He didn't want to share what they had with a snotty-nosed-kid. He liked their life just fine enough as it was. That wasn't good enough for her. They had argued over the issue numerous times, but the last straw was when she told him calmly that she didn't think it was going to work out between them. He came from a long line of successful Hawthornes and he'd be damned if he'd let her leave him.

He had to get out of this house before he succumbed to a lunatic mind. Maybe he should meet a nice girl and start having a single relationship again. Perhaps one woman's trash really was another woman's treasure...time to find out.

Steve made a phone call to an old friend of Tempest's, Brandi Loch. Brandi was twenty four years old, single, and no kids. She worked at the same bank he did, as a teller. He didn't care that she wasn't wealthy, because he was now. She was everything Tempest was not-red-haired, sweet spirited and pretty much a silent person. There wasn't anything about her that truly stuck out. She didn't have great sex appeal, but he liked that. Tempest had always overshadowed him. Brandi wouldn't. Brandi had always been attracted to him, and he knew it. But, because of her friendship with Tempest, she would never act on it. He knew this, because she had finally shared it with him after Tempest had died. Perhaps now he could convince Brandi to give them a real chance. He finally had something to really smile about, and he felt the first stirrings of hope in his chest. Yes- it was all going to work out for the best, he thought smugly.

Chapter Ten

Gentle Soul could smell the aromatic food smells from his Comanche village before it even came into view. He knew the moment Tempest spotted the small children from the village-her back stiffened, and her head snapped to attention. He bought the horse to a slow walk through the village, stopping just beside his lodge. The children chanted "*tumabi-soaitu-uno*" (curse)until he held up a hand to silence them. The men and women gathered quickly outside to greet their chief and welcome him home. He knew they wouldn't like seeing a white woman with him, but he relied on their compassion to see that Tempest would be treated well enough while here. She needed help-surely his people would understand that, once he held a meeting with the other warriors and medicine woman. Before jumping down from his horse, he made an announcement in Tempest's own language, so that she too could hear what he was saying to his people.

"My people, It has been many days since I last saw you, and I prayed the God's would sustain you while I was gone. When I was on my journey I found this white eyes in the corn fields that I often ride to. She has been wounded and she suffers memory loss and imagines she is somewhere she is not. I would not have brought her here, except for that. While she is here, I expect her to be treated as my personal guest, and ask that you show her your kindness and compassion. We are a people of longsuffering and love, are we not?" No one denied his question, so he continued. "If any one does ill towards her, the same has done it unto me. Though her skin is white, she is badly injured in her head-her thoughts..." at this being said, the children laughed openly now, and Tempest wanted to bend them each one over her knee. Instead, she listened to Gentle Soul. "Someone bring medicine woman to my lodge so that she can begin treating my guest. Her given name is Tempest. Also, I will expect the children to show her respect while she is here with us as well. Thank you my friends-that is all for now. I will hold a meeting with all warriors when I have settled Tempest in at my lodge. Thank you for hearing my words."

Tempest could see the reactions written all over their faces as Gentle Soul finished speaking. They doubted him-that much was easy to see. Tempest felt a pang of regret for Gentle Soul. Although she wasn't particularly crazy about him, she had come to trust him somewhat during their short time together. She hoped his people would trust in him as she did. She accepted his arms reaching for her, when she dismounted the horse. Again, she slid down his rock-hardened body. This time she accepted the butterflies that came with being so near him. Why not? He was after all, very beautiful.

Somebody else thought he was very beautiful too. Tempest saw the look of pure hatred upon the face of an Indian maiden. Before anybody could stop it, the maiden came up to Tempest and spat in her face. Tempest was frozen in shock at first. The Indian woman just smiled a wicked smile at her. Before she could defend herself, Gentle Soul had stepped between them and spoke harshly to the Indian maiden, as he captured both of her hands in his one. He spoke in English so Tempest could hear what he said. "Woman of Sorrow, you shame yourself by your actions to the sick woman! You bring shame to our people raising a hand to the helpless. This white woman has done nothing to deserve your spite. Go now, and hide in your lodge to ponder what evil you have done. I will pray the God's will show you mercy this day, but for now, you must leave my presence!"

"You would choose to honor a white woman over your dead wife's sister Gentle Soul?" she asked defiantly, staring a hole through Tempest as she challenged him in front of the whole village.

Tempest had heard enough. "Listen up butter cup-you may have caught me by surprise now, but I'll be ready for you next time. Spit on me again, and you'll be wearing a missing tooth in your nasty mouth. I don't want to be here anymore than you want me to be here, but I didn't have a choice. Get out of my face before I lose my religion on you Pocahontas!" without another word, Tempest walked straight into Gentle Soul's lodge as if she had always lived there. Gentle Soul smiled. He was proud of his new guest, and went inside to join her, as he waited on Medicine Woman to arrive.

Whiskey Woman

Medicine Woman was in Gentle Soul's lodge before he could retrieve the items from his horse. He spoke to her briefly before leaving her alone to check out Tempest. He explained everything that had happened in the corn field. Medicine woman was very wise, and compassionate. He trusted her to care for Tempest, and told Tempest he did. Tempest gave him a look so full of fear, he almost insisted on staying, but he wanted to give them both some privacy. Also, he could meet with the other men in his village while Tempest was being looked at.

He went to Tempest. "Whiskey woman, you will be in good hands now that Medicine Woman has arrived. I must go speak with my warriors now, and prepare them for our Buffalo hunt in a few weeks time.

Tempest didn't want to be left behind with a stranger. "I don't trust anybody here. Please stay with me Gentle Soul. You're the only person I know here."

Gentle Soul hated to see her so worried, but he had to go for now. He simply kissed her on the cheek and left his lodge and medicine woman, with Tempest. Tempest wished she could go with him, but she knew to argue now would be futile. Besides, maybe medicine woman would help her to get back home where she belonged. Medicine woman was staring at her right now.

"*Ma-ruawebukwu , hello.* Gentle Soul will return shortly. We must now see about your injuries white woman." Medicine woman directed Tempest to lie down on the soft pallet of animal furs on the floor next to the open fire pit.

"Excuse me, but I must let you know that Gentle Soul kidnapped me and will not return me home. Can you help me get home?" she watched Medicine Woman contemplate what she just said to her.

"Gentle Soul has you now *mah-tao-yo*. He will not part with you until you are better." She voiced to Tempest.

"Does this mean you believe this is a true Indian village too?" After too long a pause, she figured she did. "Pfft!" she exclaimed as she raised her hands to rest on her hips. "What's with you people?"

Whiskey Woman

Medicine woman scowled at her. "Gentle Soul right-you sick in head. Do not leave his lodge until I say you are better. Did you hit your head before Gentle Soul found you?"

Oh brother-not this again..."No. I did not hit my head, and I'm supposed to be in Kentucky." At medicine woman's blank stare she continued. "I am from Kentucky. My husband killed me and left me for dead, but I went to heaven and met with the God's and that's how I got back-through them sending me here..." She watched medicine woman's scowl deepen.

"Get rest white woman. Tomorrow we shall see if we can make you right again."

Medicine woman tried many things to help Tempest, but nothing changed. There were no medicines that would cure what Tempest had. Medicine Woman tried everything she knew to try, but nothing changed the girls mind. Frankly, Medicine Woman thought it was a bad idea for Gentle Soul to have brought her here. No white woman belonged here-sick or not. It didn't matter how much the girl tried to confide in her-she didn't like her at all, and after a while, Tempest finally got the message.

Gentle Soul had tried to give Tempest some privacy, but no amount of time alone seemed to make a difference in her healing. She still insisted that she came back from the dead and Gentle Soul was perplexed at this. After all, Tempest seemed right in her mind whenever she wasn't trying to convince him of how she had ended up in that corn field that day.

A few squaws from his village had made their way to his lodge over the next two weeks, offering Tempest advice, as well as showing her various things in their everyday life. Tempest took right up with the maidens, and she learned quickly. She now knew how to cook some, how to tan animal hides, and make bowls to eat out of. She wished Gentle Soul had a bathroom. She was tired of going in the bushes.

Although most of the Indians spoke English, there were still words Tempest heard in the Comanche tongue. Tempest learned fast though, and soon she was even trying to speak Comanche some. Gentle Soul was very proud of her and his people, for wanting to help her, even though she was a white woman.

Gentle Soul let her have run of his lodge through the day, but at night she slept next to him. The first night she hissed at him and kicked, scratched, and bit him, but he made her sleep next to him anyway. She was so tired from the journey there, that she fell asleep quickly, and never tried to fight him again over sleeping beside him at night. He was surprised she never put up a fight anymore. He knew she must trust him a little to lie beside him without being forced again, and he never abused her trust.

He began to look forward to the night, knowing he would get to feel her beside him. She was growing on him. He wondered if she felt the same way about him. It was a silly notion, but some things didn't need an explanation, and this was one of those things he supposed. He liked her, and he was pretty sure she liked him too.

It was her third night there, and Tempest came to a dreadful conclusion-she was attracted to Gentle Soul. Why else would she agree to sleep with him? They both lay on their sides facing one another when he smiled and winked at her. She giggled in response.

"Why are you staring at me?" she asked him.

His eyes were black as onyx and she felt them pull her.

"Because you are beautiful and this warrior likes looking at your beauty."

Tempest didn't know how to respond to that, so she just acted like he never said it.

"Why do you keep me here, instead of taking me home?"

Gentle Soul thought on that for a moment before answering. "I cannot let you go until I know your mind is right."

"I could run when you're gone during the day..."

"Only a fool would leave this camp Whiskey, and you already know what happens when you leave me..." he reminded her. "Besides, I would find you and bring you back-maybe even whip good sense into you."

Tempest huffed angrily and rolled over to sleep. She quickly figured out that she wasn't going anywhere until Gentle Soul thought she was better in the head. She had never cow-tailed down to a man in her life, but she had to depend on Gentle Soul for everything now. Her life had come to a stand-still since meeting Gentle Soul. She wondered what it would take for him to believe her. He certainly had no right to judge her story when his was just as crazy. He might not be with the village people band, but why did he insist he was a Comanche chief? It made no sense to her-none at all. If he wasn't really an Indian, how could all these other Indians be explained? Soon, she would do some exploring on her on among the people here...

Since Tempest wasn't allowed to leave the lodge except to relieve herself in the bushes, Gentle Soul brought her fresh water to wash herself with every night, until she was trusted to bathe at the river. It wasn't the same as a bathtub, but Tempest made use of it anyway. She soon fell into a routine each day and it wasn't all that bad. She could think of worse states to be in than being the captive of a sexy man who looked like an Indian and acted like one. No doubt about it-he was a hottie!

Several women of the village brought doeskin dresses to Tempest, and it thrilled Gentle Soul to see her start wearing them. He started to wonder what it would be like to have her as his woman, but knew he could not if she was sick, and surely she was. This troubled him greatly. He wished he could make her well again. He marveled at what she had told him about her husband killing her. He wondered if she even realized how impossible it was-saying she went to heaven, and was sent back here-in an earlier time that she was used to.

The hot summer days were now turning slightly chilly, and that meant it would soon be time to hunt food for his village to sustain them through the winter months. This time of year was always exciting and welcomed by his people.

Everyone but Woman of Sorrow seemed to welcome their guest, Tempest. In fact, Tempest remained the talk for the coming weeks there. He had watched her go from weary to curious about his people, and it made him smile. He liked watching her in the midst of his people-most seemed to accept her here as a mere extension from him. His people were a loving people for sure. Even the children welcomed her here. He watched her play with some of the children and he wondered how she would look with her belly swollen with child...to be exact-his child. He'd be willing to wager that most men in the village had wondered the same thing, but it made him angry to think of anyone with her except him.

Medicine woman couldn't figure out a cure for Tempest, and it troubled him greatly. All he could do now was pray to the Gods to make her whole again. Surely the Gods would help her now. He felt like a newborn pup around her-with him doing all the following, and her leading the way. He was a chief, and a warrior. So why wasn't he acting like one? Perhaps it was her natural beauty that kidnapped his mind when he was around her. He knew one thing for certain: He didn't want anyone but her to warm his blankets with at night. She may've kept her distance during the day, but at night, even in sleep, her body sought out his warmth and comfort, and that made all of this foolishness worth it to him.

Tempest studied her surroundings. Medicine woman had told her to go to sleep, but she just couldn't sleep this night. She didn't trust anyone here accept Gentle Soul. As she looked around his lodge, which was very spacious indeed, she noticed how old everything seemed to be, and wondered if it meant something, or if it was just the way he lived as an Indian. By now, she had somehow accepted that he truly was an Indian. But she couldn't understand why he insisted that she needed to be helped. She needed to find something to prove she was right, and that the year was 2003. She wondered if Gentle Soul was as sick in the head as he presumed her to be. This was all nonsense. She needed to get back to Kentucky, and confront Steve. She didn't feel wanted here, or comfortable, but what could she do?

Gentle Soul had discussed the plans for him and his warriors to leave for the hunting party within the next few days. Dancing Eyes was his best friend, and he could very well see his friends eyes dancing as he spoke to his men about helping Tempest. Dancing eyes was more like a brother than a best friend to Gentle Soul, and he took advantage of the relationship now to pick fun at Gentle Soul.

"Gentle Soul, the white woman is surely sick in the head if she came here with you", He joked.

Whiskey Woman

Gentle Soul laughed deep in his chest at his friend. "Dancing Eyes makes me laugh like a child of ten summers. Get your bow ready for the hunt, and shut the hole in your gaping mouth before I shut it for you," he teased back. They both laughed-neither one would ever lay a hand on the other, and they would die for each other if needed. It was Dancing Eyes who stood by him when his parents died, and Dancing Eyes again, when his wife and brother died in the ambush against his people.

"It is good to see you laugh again Gentle Soul. Your people have missed seeing you so."

"It is good to be able to laugh again Dancing Eyes. I never thought I'd be laughing again-ever."

"What are you going to do with the white woman?" Gentle Eyes asked reluctantly.

Gentle Soul had no idea what he was going to do with Tempest. He hoped medicine woman had strong enough medicine to help her so he could be done with her, and take her to her home. She was too distracting to look upon, and yet, he looked upon her many times since they had been thrown together by fate. Woman of Sorrow had vexed him greatly by her actions. He supposed that was his entire fault though. Ever since Silent Speaks died, he had taken care of Woman of Sorrow. Looking back on it now, he could finally see his mistake. She thought more of him than just a protector and provider. He needed to put an end to her jealousy now, before she got out of hand.

"Dancing Eyes, I need a favor…" he spoke to his best friend.

Dancing Eyes grew serious. "Anything…"

Gentle Soul knew he'd say that. He was a good man and warrior. "Woman of Sorrow needs a provider and protector. She has taken advantage of my generosity and I need to put distance between us. Would you care for her Dancing Eyes?"

Dancing Eyes never wavered. "It would be an honor to care for her as mine own. I will spend time with her, until I can call her my woman." He said solemnly.

Whiskey Woman

Gentle Soul was well pleased at this. "Thank you, my friend, and my brother. It is good."

Chapter Eleven

Tempest awoke with a start. Gentle Soul was already gone, and Medicine Woman was cooking something on the fire that smelled horrible. She hoped whatever it was wasn't meant for her. She stretched and sat up. "Hello Medicine Woman; What are you fixing?"

Medicine Woman grunted and looked back at Tempest for a moment. "I'm fixing something that may help your memory. This is our last resort White woman-I don't know of anything else to do after this."

Tempest noticed her expression and felt compassion for her. All of this was her fault. Well, it was mostly the Gods fault, but she couldn't very well say that, could she? Medicine Woman already thought she was crazy; she didn't need to add to that.

Medicine Woman dipped a ladle into the soup and put it in a crudely-fashioned bowl for Tempest. It smelled so bad that Tempest pinched her nose while she drank. Medicine Woman smiled her approval when Tempest had drained the entire bowl.

"Medicine Woman, I need to take a bath. Is there a bathtub around here?"

Medicine Woman sighed heavily. "I don't know what you're talking about Tempest, but we bathe in the river. Gentle Soul says you can bathe in the river now, as long as I go with you. Let me gather you some clothes and soap." She held out everything she had gathered for Tempest to take.

"What are the two bottles here?"

"One is goat milk soap, and the other is raspberry scented water for your hair."

"Where is the river?"

Whiskey Woman

"I will take you there. Follow me."

Medicine Woman and Tempest both came out of the lodge and it was Tempest's first time beyond it. Children were playing outside with their mothers, and all looked upon her with quiet surprise. One of the children came up to Tempest and offered her a handful of weeds. Tempest took them in one hand and smiled at the small little girl. She couldn't be more than three years old and she had the fullest head of black hair Tempest had ever seen on a child. She was precious. She seemed to take up with Tempest, and her skin color didn't bother the little girl either. Tempest felt her heart tug for the small child who now reached for her hand, and Tempest took it in hers.

Medicine Woman spoke to the child with words Tempest didn't understand, and suddenly the child burst into tears and ran away from Tempest to return to her mother's arms. Tempest felt great disappointment.

"What did you say to her?" she asked Medicine Woman.

"I told her not to bother the white eyes, or she may get sick in head like you."

Tempest was truly hurt. As much time as she had spent with Medicine Woman, she thought that they had become somewhat friendly with one another. Now she knew better. These people would never accept her into their lives, and the thought made her tear up, but she didn't dare let herself succumb to the desire to shed her tears in front of Medicine Woman, or the other women watching their interaction.

Tempest stood ramrod straight and pursed her lips together in anger. "You may go now Medicine Woman. I have no desire to keep you with me any longer."

"Gentle Soul is our chief, and he told me to watch after you while he was gone on the great hunt today. So I will stay with you."

Tempest knew it would do no good to argue with the stubborn woman, so she just kept walking towards the river. Just up ahead ten more foot was the river. It was a beautiful sunny day out today, and the birds

Whiskey Woman

were singing and chirping happily. Tempest kept replaying the image of the little girl who Medicine Woman had hurt with her words. She couldn't shake her anger, so she decided to use it instead. Besides, it was obvious they all thought she was crazy, why not go with it?

Tempest shed her clothing and walked into the water with the two bottles in her left hand. Once she was waist deep in the cold water, she ducked underneath to get her hair wet. She turned her back to Medicine Woman and scrubbed her body good with the soap, before washing her hair with it as well. Next, she poured the scented water over her hair and the remainder over her body. She decided to mess with Medicine Woman before she got out.

Tempest let go of both bottles and raised her two hands up as high in the air as they would go, while chanting a diddy she had learned in choir. "Do re me fa so la te do..." She had to contain her laughter once she saw Medicine Woman's face.

Medicine Woman couldn't believe what she was seeing and hearing. The white woman was talking in a language she had never heard before and she couldn't make out what was being said either. This scared her, as she began to think that maybe this white woman was really a witch, or worse, someone the Gods had sent to vex them all. She lifted her own voice in prayer to the Gods and prayed, "Father help us be rid of this strange woman-please..." The more she prayed, the louder Tempest cried her own prayers. She turned and quickly ran to the village to get a few witnesses. When she came back Tempest was sitting on a nearby rock fully-clothed and running her fingers through her long hair.

Woman of Sorrow was among the many women she had bought with her. "What do you wish us to see Medicine Woman? The white woman has only bathed and is now combing through her hair. You said she was chanting a spell upon us, but I hear no words from her mouth..."

Medicine woman felt like a fool. She glared at Tempest as the others walked back to their lodges. Tempest gave her a wink and a smile. This idiot was going to be trouble, she just knew it!

On the way back to Gentle Soul's lodge, Tempest finally spoke to Medicine Woman. "Tell others to shun me again, and I promise you my next act will make today's look like you're smart. She didn't have to ask Medicine Woman to leave this time, because she angrily stomped off towards her own lodge, leaving Tempest alone finally. For the first time since being there, Tempest giggled as she made her way to Gentle Soul's lodge. Once inside, she grew restless. So, she decided to do some cleaning to keep herself busy. Unfortunately, she could find nothing to clean with. She finally just contented herself by straightening up. The lodge was too dark for her taste, so she left and walked around in the nearby fields, picking wildflowers. After she had gathered more than enough, she went back and found something to place them in, and opened a nearby flap which acted like a window in the center wall of the lodge. She smiled. It already looked and felt better with a slight woman's touch. She hated being cooped up here waiting on Gentle Soul to return from the hunt, because he would be gone for two more days, according to Medicine Woman.

Tempest saw a shadow at the front of the lodge's door and went to open it. The little Indian girl was standing there sucking on her thumb. "Well, what do we have here?" Tempest asked her, but the girl remained silent, just watching her. Tempest knew she must be curious, but also scared a little. She left the door open and went over to the fireplace and waited, as the little girl followed her inside.

"My name is Tempest. What is your name?"

"Little Doe." The small child answered her solemnly.

"Ahh, that is quite a lovely name to have Miss Little Doe. Is your thumb good?" she teased her.

Little Does reached her thumb out for Tempest to admire. "It does look awfully good…" she confessed to Little Doe. Little Doe smiled her appreciation.

"Are you hungry Little Doe?"

Little Doe nodded her head up and down for Tempest.

"Well then, let me see what I can make for us to eat. I'm rather hungry myself."

Whiskey Woman

Tempest pointed to the pine bedding and asked Little Doe if she'd like to sit on the bed while she made them some dinner. Little Doe ran quickly to it and flopped down upon it. Tempest found some meal and water and made them some cornbread to go with the remainder of corn they still had. Once it was done, she ladled out a bowl for each of them and came to sit beside Little Doe to eat with her.

Once dinner was finished Tempest taught Little Doe how to play patty-cake and they played patty cake for over an hour before there was a knock at her door. A young Indian woman stood there and scanned the room once Tempest opened the door. After spotting Little Doe, the woman motioned for the child to come with her. Little Doe clung to Tempests' legs in fear of the woman, and Tempest wondered what had happened to make the child so scared of her. She had no choice but to let the woman take Little Doe, as she was convinced this woman must be her mother. The mother spoke rapidly to the little girl and when Little Doe tried to move back from her, the woman grabbed her arm painfully and gave it a hard jerk. Little Doe cried aloud in pain and pulled her dress up to show Tempest her bloody backside that had been beaten. Tempest also saw the bruising on the little girl's back. Tempest knew she had to do something. Tempest placed one hand around each wrist of the Mother and held on for dear life as she waited for Little Doe to come stand behind her. The maiden hissed at Tempest and brought her hands up to get out of Tempest's hold. She shook her arms hard and Tempest fell backwards. Once on the floor of the lodge, Tempest saw black spots and knew she was close to passing out, but she'd be damned if she let this shell of a woman take Little Doe and more than likely, hurt her. She swept a leg out and fell the Indian woman, so that they both lay upon the ground of the lodge floor. Little Doe was crying in fear, and Tempest knew she couldn't let this go on any longer. So, she sat up, facing the woman and clenched her fist up tightly before punching her as hard as she could. It worked. The mother slumped back to the floor completely. She was out for a bit.

Tempest gathered Little Doe in her arms and struggled to get to her feet. She was dizzy, but she finally made it up. Without worrying how it would look, Tempest carried Little Doe outside and cleared her throat for all to hear her. "My name is Tempest, not white eyes, or white woman! Tempest! Somebody needs to come get the sorry excuse for a Mother out of my lodge before I hurt her badly. She has scared her own child silly, and I challenge anybody here to try and take her away from me. She will remain with me until Gentle Soul comes back from the hunt."

Medicine Woman stepped forward. "You can't take a mothers child from her white eyes. Gentle Soul will surely punish your actions against his people, wait and see..." she sneered.

It took three women to carry out Little Does mother from the lodge. Tempest had heard more than enough bullshit from Medicine Woman, and she picked Little Doe up and raised her dress to show her bruised little body. Everyone gasped-shocked to see one of their own do such a terrible thing and to a small child no less!

Tempest shook with her rage. "Like I said, I will challenge ANYONE who tries to take Little Doe away from me." Everyone stood silent, and some hung their heads in shame at what they had seen. Nobody challenged her though, and after everyone went back to their own lodges, Tempest carried Little Doe in and laid her upon the bed Gentle Soul had made for them. She would keep Little Doe sleeping with her until Gentle Soul came home. The little girl snuggled closer to Tempest and offered Tempest her thumb. Tempest smiled and she began weaving a magical bedtime story for Little Doe. Within minutes, both of them were fast asleep.

Just outside Gentle Souls lodge, Medicine Woman held a sack that contained poisonous berries. If enough were eaten, they could be deadly. This made the second time the white woman had made her look bad in front of her people, and she must pay for that. Gentle Soul was a weak chief now that he had brought her to their village. After she was gone, maybe their village would get back to how it used to be before the white eyes had come. She smiled as she walked back to her own lodge. Tomorrow she would make sure the white eyes ate the poisonous berries.

Hunting Party

Gentle Soul lead his men high upon the land from one side to another, enclosing the buffalo that were grazing there, and ensuring they would kill as many as possible this day. It had only been two days since he had left Tempest, but he missed her terribly, and thought of her often. He felt uneasy about leaving her behind, but he knew that Medicine Woman would take good care of her. After all, hadn't he taken care of Medicine Woman through the years after the death of Smiling Eyes, her late husband? He had led his men to many deer the previous day, so they were ahead in their hunt. If things went well, he could return home tomorrow, a day earlier than planned. He prayed to the Gods it would.

Chapter Twelve

Tempest felt Little Doe squirm beside her early the next morning, so she got up and led the little girl to the nearby bushes to use the bathroom. The two of them walked down to the river to gather water and after Tempest rinsed her mouth out and washed her face off, she did the same for Little Doe. She held Little Doe's hand in hers and led the way back to the village, and their lodge.

She knew Little Doe must be hungry, so she got a bowl out and asked her to come with her to hunt berries. Finding the berries proved harder than she thought it would be. She came back nearly empty-handed, and she chewed her bottom lip worrying over what to fix for breakfast. She didn't have to worry long. Medicine Woman asked to step into the lodge, and Tempest started to deny her, until Medicine Woman apologized. She then stepped to the side to let her enter the lodge. Medicine woman held a big bowl of something steamy, and it smelled heavenly. "I make berry soup for you and bring nuts and cornbread for Little Doe, to say I am sorry..."

Tempest was impressed, and humbled by the offering. "Thank you so much Medicine Woman. We shall eat it now, if that's okay with you? Medicine Woman smiled warmly for the first time. "Berries give Little Doe rash. She eat cornbread, and you eat berry soup." She said.

"Alright then. I will; thank you Medicine Woman. Would you like to eat with us? There's a lot here."

"No. I have already eaten this morning, but thank you."

Tempest gave Little Doe her breakfast and then sat down to eat her berry soup. It smelled quite delicious and she didn't want to hurt Medicine Woman's feelings, so she ate some of it, and then set the bowl aside.

Whiskey Woman

"You must eat it all white, er...Tempest, that is....please. I worked very hard on getting it just right for you."

Tempest felt a pang of guilt and grabbed the unfinished bowl of berry soup. "Yes, of course you did. Forgive me Medicine Woman. I shall eat every last drop." Tempest downed the rest of the soup before handing the empty bowl back to a beaming Medicine Woman.

Little Doe was shaking her head no, and pointing to the soup bowl that was empty now. "What is it Little Doe?" You can't eat this honey-it gives you a rash..."

Little Doe still pointed to the empty bowl and shook her head as if to say "No." Tempest supposed the little girl was just confused. After all, a lot had happened in just two days time.

Medicine Woman stared at Little Doe as if she wanted to shut her up, and Tempest didn't miss the withering look she gave Little Doe. Her hackles rose at this. "Medicine Woman, I don't understand you. You're mean-spirited to this child, and then come apologize to me, and then make faces at her this morning. What in the world has come over you?"

Before Medicine Woman could answer, Tempest became swimmy-headed and her vision was blurring. "Medicine Woman, I think I may be sick..." and with that confession, she began to violently vomit. "Please help me..." she implored her, but Medicine Woman was smiling the happiest smile she had ever displayed to Tempest, and Tempest knew then, that she had been poisoned.

Little Doe ran to the nearby lodge of Loving Heart. Loving heart was an elderly woman whose husband had died many years ago, and who had never been blessed with children. Loving heart loved the Cheyenne people, and felt blessed to know Gentle Soul as good as the son she never had. She had become somewhat of a surrogate Mother to Gentle Soul, after the death of both of his parents, and the tribe respected her greatly because of it. Little Doe was urgently trying to get her to go with her somewhere, so Loving Heart took the child's hand and let her lead her to Gentle Soul's lodge. What she found inside made her skin crawl ominously in foreboding. There, lying atop a makeshift bed of pine needles lay the white woman named Tempest. She was convulsing badly. Medicine Woman had been seen departing the lodge before Loving Heart could make her way inside. Now she knew why. Medicine Woman had a hand in whatever was wrong with the white woman, and it didn't look good at all.

Little Doe stood beside Tempest and cried pitifully. It tore at Loving Heart's very soul. Knowing the child loved this woman so much, in such little time, told her all she needed to know about Tempest. She must get to work immediately, if she were going to try and save the young woman from death. She spoke to Little Doe rapidly, in terms the child might understand, and was rewarded with the little girl's obedience. Little Doe fetched water and plenty of blankets for them. Though the child was small, she was very strong. She had heard about what Little Doe's Mother did to her, and she felt her own heart swell with compassion for the white woman, for taking up for a child that wasn't hers, and taking the child into her home. In that way, she felt a real kinship with Tempest. She prayed the Gods would help the young woman through this.

Little Doe brought the empty berry bowl to Loving Heart and pointed at it, and then to Tempest's mouth. Loving Heart inspected the bowl and could clearly see the stain left by the berries, and she immediately knew what had happened. "Little Doe, did Tempest eat all the berries?"

Little Doe shook her head up and down.

"Did Medicine Woman give this to Tempest?"

Again, Little Doe shook her head up and down.

Loving Heart swallowed the lump of fear in her throat. Without the help of the Gods, Tempest would surely die. Those berries were more poisonous than a snake bite. Loving Heart boiled water, and sent Little Doe out to get a few needed things from her lodge. Little Doe was fast and she obeyed without balking or whining.

Tempest became feverish and the pain in her belly rapidly increased so much, she thought she would surely die. Thankfully, she blacked out several times while Loving Heart did her best to nurse her through it all. Tempest saw the fear in Little Doe's eyes and she took the child's hands in hers and kissed them before returning back into oblivion.

Whiskey Woman

She didn't recognize the elderly lady that was trying to help her, but she hoped she lived long enough to thank her.

Every time she started to fall asleep, Loving Heart made her drink something so foul she vomited over and over again. This went on throughout the entire night, up until the breaking of a new dawn. Finally, Loving Heart told her to get some much needed rest. She went to sleep immediately. She woke up several hours later only to have to drink that awful drink again. Once again, she spent a good hour vomiting before she was allowed to rest again. She knew she was getting delirious when she heard the voice of Gentle Soul begging her to come back to him. She smiled, happy that he was in her dreams. "Don't worry Gentle Soul; I will tell the Gods about how nice you were to me..."

"No Whiskey! You must stay here with me." Gentle Soul could see her eyes closing and it scared him greatly. "Please don't leave me Whiskey..." he pleaded.

"Take care of Little Doe. Don't let her Mother have her back...and thank Loving Heart for me. She helped me when Medicine Woman poisoned me."

Gentle Soul looked to Loving Heart. "Is this true? Did Medicine Woman poison her?"

"Yes. I saw her leave myself Gentle Soul, but now is not the time for vengeance. I've done all I can do for her. It's up to the Gods now. Pray Gentle Soul. I will be back later to check on her, but I must get some rest too, and I will take Little Doe to my lodge so you can have some privacy."

Gentle Soul thanked her.

"One last thing Gentle Soul-your woman is very strong willed. This may be to her advantage now. She saved the child from the abuse of her Mother. Little Doe loves her already. Please don't get angry with her over taking the child as her own. She did what any real mother would do..." and with that final word, she took Little Doe and left.

Gentle Soul prayed with all his might that Tempest would come out of this. She had to. He felt guilty that he wasn't here to protect her-especially after she told him he was the only person that she did trust. He had let her down. He heated some water and undressed her. He took time and bathed her as best as he could and dressed her before covering her up with a blanket. He sat beside her and lightly stroked her face as he prayed to the Gods for her recovery. Medicine Woman would pay for this. He had warned his people from the beginning.

Tempest talked in her sleep. "Little Doe, don't go back to her..."

"...you can't have her."

"Where are you Gentle Soul?"

Gentle Soul lay beside her and whispered in her ear. "I'm right here Whiskey Woman and I'm not leaving until you're better. I am so sorry love...I'll never leave you alone again." He hoped she could hear his words.

Loving Heart and Little Doe came that evening. Gentle Soul was amazed by what he saw. Little Doe came running to Tempest and fell down beside her with tears running down her tiny face.

"Tempi...Tempi...wake up!" she pleaded.

Gentle Soul and Loving Heart watched in amazement as Tempest finally opened her eyes for the child and whispered, "Yes Little Doe, Tempi hears you now. Come lay with me..."

Little Doe smiled the biggest smile he'd ever seen then, and quickly laid down with her, content to play with Tempest's long hair while Tempest drifted asleep again. Everyone smiled. This was a good sign that Tempest would make it now, and Gentle Soul thanked the Gods for not taking her from him. He asked Loving Heart to stay with them while he took care of Medicine Woman.

Chapter Thirteen

Two days later Tempest woke up to find Little Doe in between her and Gentle Soul. She smiled. She hoped she wasn't dreaming again. She whispered, "Gentle Soul, are you really here? She watched his eyes open and he raised a hand to lightly stroke her cheek over Little Doe. "Yes Whiskey, I am really here, and so is your daughter." He watched her reaction and he smiled his pleasure to see her smile bigger than ever.

"*Daughter?*" A lump lodged in her throat. "Little Doe is *mine*? What about her mother? What about her? Won't she hate me if I take her?"

Gentle Soul grew serious. "Her mother gave up her rights when she struck her, and Little Doe loves you, she already thinks of you as her *Pia*."

"Gentle Soul, may I ask you to do something for me, please?"

"Anything." He readily answered her.

"It's a pretty big favor…."

"Anything for you Whiskey…just ask."

"If something should happen to me, would you promise me that you'd raise Little Doe and love her?"

Gentle Soul could see she was worried. "Of course I would Whiskey, but nothing is going to happen to you again. I'm here now, and I won't leave you by yourself."

"What happened to Medicine Woman?"

"Medicine Woman admitted what she had done to you and I took her myself, out of our village. She is no longer in my care or good graces."

"I'm sorry Gentle Soul. I hate to hear that, but for Little Doe's sake, I'm glad she's gone. Thank you." Tempest reached up and lightly kissed Gentle Soul's cheek.

"Never thank me for caring for you. You are my woman, and you will always come first-Little Doe too. I will teach her how to ride and hunt as good as any man, or better."

"Oh Gentle Soul, you are a good man. Any woman would be blessed to have you." She said before she thought.

Gentle Soul pierced her with his eyes. "And you, Whiskey? Would you be blessed to have me?"

Tempest knew she had made a big mistake by saying that, but it was too late now to take it back. She knew, for his sake, she had better get this right.

"If I were looking, then yes, I would be blessed, but I am content to be on my own Gentle Soul, with Little Doe." She could see how her words hurt him, and she wished she could take them back, but the Gods didn't want them to be together, and she couldn't help that any more than he could. She just wished he could understand her reasons for pushing him away. Her words cut him deeply. Gentle Soul didn't say another word. There was no use to.

Chapter Fourteen

It had been a week since her poisoning. Tempest was enjoying her new daughter, every day, but she missed Gentle Soul. He hadn't left her alone, true to his word, but no matter how nice some of the people were, she missed Gentle Soul. He had kept his distance during the day, ever since that night he had asked her if she was blessed. She had hurt him, and she felt badly for that, but she didn't see any other way for them. Besides, she needed to get back to her life.

Gentle Soul was there every night, and they slept with Little Doe in between them. Although they never talked, Gentle Soul always had his arm over her and Little Doe. No matter how badly she had disappointed him, he would protect them both. How she wished things could be different between them, but Gentle Soul couldn't even admit what year they were in. He insisted something was wrong with her, but she thought something was wrong with him and his people. Maybe they had suffered a trauma over being forced to leave their lands long ago…she wished he could see the truth.

Tempest spent the next day playing with Little Doe and teaching her a few words. Night had descended on them quickly and after they had dinner Tempest told Little Doe more stories until she fell asleep. Tempest was still awake when Gentle Soul made his way back home. It was silly, but she was glad to see him again. She had missed him. She was probably only missing him because of her dependence on him, she thought. It had nothing to do with how beautiful he was standing there by the fire and looking at her through hooded eyes. It had nothing to do with how he had stood up for her against Woman of Sorrow and Medicine Woman either.

Gentle Soul walked over to the fireplace and made him a plate of food. He watched Tempest switch between standing on each foot. She was nervous about something, but what?

"Whiskey Woman, why are you nervous in front of me? Do you not know that I would never hurt you?"

"I don't think you would Gentle Soul, but I'm not comfortable here. I need to get back to my own home."

Gentle Soul attended the food and didn't bother looking up at her. "This will be your home until you are well enough to travel Whiskey."

"But..." she started.

"No more foolish talk. I must eat now."

"But I'll never get better according to you, if you insist on pretending this is all real. If you truly are the Indian you claim to be, then what does that really mean? This is the 20th century, not the 15th Gentle Soul. Please help me understand why you can't see that..."

Gentle Soul was out of words. Instead, he went to a corner of the open lodge and took a box out and picked through its contents until he finally wrapped his hands around a newspaper he had saved from the ambush on his village. The missionary had brought it to him long ago. He laid the paper down on the roughly made table and pointed at the date on it, for her to see. "Look Whiskey, this is from two years ago, when my people were ambushed. Pay attention to the date." He offered her.

Tempest looked at the paper. The headlines blared back at her. "Indian village attacked...death toll rises to over 200." It was dated for 1865...Tempest shrank away, and began screeching, "Nooo...there's no way. This can't be true! Oh my God! Oh God, please help me to understand this..."

Gentle Soul watched her slip down to the floor, as if she were too tired to stand another second. He could tell the news devastated her, and he felt badly for her. He sank to the floor with her and reached over to hold her now shaking body against him. "Oh Whiskey, I am so sorry to upset you, but you must accept the truth of this." Tempest held onto Gentle Soul until she could cry no more. After a little while Gentle Soul stood, while pulling her up with him, but she wasn't ready to move away from him yet. So, he stood in place and waited.

Whiskey Woman

"What state are we in again Gentle Soul?" She whispered against his shoulder.

"We are in Oklahoma Whiskey." He said.

"Oklahoma..." She whispered, clearly stunned.

Gentle Soul wished he could make her feel better about all of this, but all he could do was send up a silent prayer to the God's., and he did.

Tempest had had enough already. This wasn't funny-at all! *Did the God's think it was funny to send her back in time? And what about getting revenge on Steve?? Why the hell send her to an Indian man of all scenarios' she could've been in?* Tempest was not amused any longer.

"What are you thinking Whiskey?" Gentle Soul asked her, sincerely troubled to see her crying. He hated to see any woman cry, but watching this woman cry tore his heart out. He raised his hands to cup her face in them, while watching her eyes slowly focus on him. She looked like a small child that was hurt. He wished he could comfort her.

"What am I thinking? Do you really want to know that Gentle Soul?" she asked with her heart in her eyes.

"Yes, Whiskey, I do." He assured her.

Tempest knew if she told him he'd never believe it. Hadn't she already tried telling him the truth? He thought her to be crazy then. What would he think now? She wasn't ready to find out now, no matter how much she wanted to. "I'm wondering how long I could stay here Gentle Soul. It looks like I have nowhere else to go now that I've realized how wrong I was about having a home somewhere else."

Gentle Soul wrapped his arms around her again, to reassure her. "Whiskey, you are welcome to stay as long as you need to."

His generosity humbled her hard heart. "But, what about your people? What about Woman of Sorrow?" she hedged.

"I am the Chief among my people Whiskey. As long as I am a good protector and provider to my people, no one will say anything to you. I am sorry about what happened with Woman of Sorrow, but that will not be happening again." He assured her.

"Where would I stay?"

"You will stay with me, and be my woman Whiskey. It is my bed you will warm."

"I'm not going to be your lover Gentle Soul, no matter how nice you are. Besides, a woman likes to be courted, ya' know what I mean?"

Gentle Soul laughed. "Whiskey, I believe the Gods sent you to me, and no-not just my lover Whiskey-I want you to become my wife."

Chapter Fifteen

"You want what?" Tempest knew she must've heard him wrong. "It sounded like you said you wanted me to be your wife." She laughed.

Gentle Soul winced. "That's exactly what I said."

"I can't be your wife! We barely know each other!" she exclaimed.

"You are not well, have no husband, or anyone else to provide and protect you."

"I don't need all that. I'm a successful writer ya know..."

"And how much money do you have to start building your new home? Where is your food? Your furnishings? Where are clothes for you?"

Tempest didn't want to face anything else right now. "Why would you want a woman who could offer you nothing Gentle Soul?"

"I never said those things. You have fire in your eyes, and in your blood. You're brave, and *nai-bi beautiful*. That's a good start for me."

Tempest didn't know what to say to this. All this time she had thought he was a member of a band. But no-he was a chief of the Cheyenne tribe. The Gods must be messing with her. They must've thought this would be funny, but it wasn't funny at all. Gentle Soul was not part of their game. He was sincere in his offer. This was crazy! How could she marry a man she didn't know, after marrying a man she thought she knew too well, and been killed because she was wrong about that one?

Gentle Soul let her go and walked over to the large pallet of animal covers. He looked hurt. "Come my woman, we must rest this night, for there will be plenty to do tomorrow." Tempest decided sleep would be a welcome thing now, so she joined him on the floor, and even lay beside him without arguing.

"Gentle Soul, may I have a few days to consider your proposal?"

"Yes Whiskey-now sleep. I will chase away your bad dreams."

Tempest didn't argue. After all she'd been through; it would be more surprising if she didn't have bad dreams. Besides, she never argued that she wasn't attracted to Gentle Soul. He was after all, a Cheyenne chief and warrior. Even now, she could feel the hardness of his body through her dress. She wanted to touch him, feel his kiss on her lips...yep! Tonight was going to be hard.

"What are you thinking so much on Whiskey?"

"I was just thinking I'd like to kiss you Gentle Soul, but I'm supposed to be a good woman."

Gentle Soul laughed aloud at her confession, and turned her to face him on her side. "Gentle Soul thinks you are a great woman. Now kiss me my Whiskey Woman! He begged her softly.

Tempest didn't falter with his request. In an instant her mouth found his, and she kissed him hungrily. His mouth was heavenly, just like she thought it would be. Maybe being a squaw wasn't so bad, she thought...and when he kissed her back, she thought being his wife might be a good thing too.

Heaven

Destiny was pacing back and forth. She had to check in with the Gods today, and she dreaded it. Tempest was supposed to be fighting a union between her and Gentle Soul. Instead, she was falling in love with him, and didn't even know it. How would the Gods react to this news she wondered. She knew this one was going to be trouble from the very beginning. Why couldn't she have worked at hells gates? It was time to meet the Gods now, and she took a deep breath, rolled her eyes again and went in to face them.

The God of Love spoke first. "Just because you don't agree with my decision concerning Tempests' love life, it doesn't make it less real. I gave both her and Gentle Soul exactly what they asked for, and soon enough, they will realize it."

"But God of Love, how will this ever work? They barely know each other."

"Love knows no distance or time frame Destiny. You're an angel, you wouldn't understand."

"Okay. Does this also mean she will be allowed to stay with him, until he dies, before coming back to Heaven?" Destiny was concerned for Tempest.

The God of Judgment now spoke. "No. Tempest will have to be present to see what I do with her husband."

"But what about Gentle Soul? Don't you think they've both suffered enough? If she leaves him, he'll be shattered, especially after the death of his wife."

The God of Life spoke up. "We decided to let her go back for a mission. That's all. After the mission is complete, she will return back to heaven for eternity. That is her future-not Gentle Soul."

Destiny knew it was futile to argue with any of them, so she didn't. After she was excused, she walked back out of the throne room to ponder everything that was said. Angels weren't supposed to feel, but her heart felt very heavy with sadness. She would have to visit Tempest and warn her against loving Gentle Soul. Sometimes, she hated being an angel...

Destiny transported herself to where Tempest lay sleeping. She looked so peaceful, she hated to awaken her, but she had to, and now was the best time, while Gentle Soul was asleep. She floated in front of Tempest and caused a butterfly to land on Tempests' nose. Tempest awoke immediately to swat it away, and froze when she saw Destiny.

"Go away Destiny."

"No Tempest-we must talk. I have news for you from the Gods. Just let me come closer and whisper in your ear, so Gentle Soul doesn't wake up."

"Fine, but hurry Destiny! I'm enjoying the warrior way too much." Tempest actually smiled.

As much as Destiny hated to, she knew she had to tell Tempest the truth, even though it would only hurt her. So, she leaned down into Tempest ear and whispered the whole conversation into her ear." When she was finished, Tempests' face was red with anger, using it to mask her hurt.

"No. They can't do this! They were the ones who sent me here Destiny. Tell them hell no!!! I'm not going back to Steve, or Heaven. I want to stay with Gentle Soul. Please tell them Destiny..." she pleaded with Destiny.

"Tempest, I tried to tell them, but their minds are set. I can't stay. I just wanted to warn you. Don't get too close to Gentle Soul, because you can't have him. Don't forget-you're still married to Steve, and Tempest...do not make the Gods angry with you. You can't win that way..." and with that, Destiny disappeared before Tempests' eyes.

Tempest lay in the dark and thought of everything she had been through. Life wasn't fair. She didn't understand why she had to be present when The Gods decided what to do with Steve. She could care less now. Besides, wasn't one of the Gods the God of Love?? She may not know Gentle Soul enough to actually love him, but why couldn't she explore it and see? This all must be coming from the God of Judgment. What had she done so evil to be denied this chance at love, and why should she care if she was still married to the man who killed her? She didn't owe him anything, but apparently the Gods felt she should at least be divorced.

What about Gentle Soul? Surely he had suffered too much already. All he wanted was to be with her. It wasn't asking for much, was it? How could she tell him this, when he didn't even believe what she had already tried to tell him when they met? He would never believe her. He would think her sicker than he thought her to be right now.

She knew what she had to do. She didn't want to hurt Gentle Soul, so she knew she must make him so angry at her, he'd change his mind about wanting to marry her. It shouldn't be hard; she seemed to know how to push a man's buttons. She would have to harden her heart against him, if she was to be believed though. Gentle Soul had a calming way about him that made you want to melt into his arms. When she thought of Little Doe, her stomach churned. She was no better than the child's real Mother, by leaving her behind, but she knew she didn't have a future now, so she had to make the best decision based on that.

While Gentle Soul slept, Tempest tried to think of a way to get away from him. If she succeeded, he'd be mad as hell at her, and that's exactly what she wanted. She suddenly thought of a way that might work. Woman of Sorrow would be too happy to see her leave, so she knew that she must find her and see if she could leave while Gentle Soul was still sleeping. She felt a pang of jealousy rip through her at the possibility that Gentle Soul might end up with Woman of Sorrow.

Twenty minutes later, she had found the right lodge, without Gentle Soul chasing after her. Woman of Sorrow wasn't happy to see her, until she told her she had to leave here. For the first time, Tempest saw the squaw smile. She was actually pretty when she smiled, which only irked her more when she thought about the squaw with Gentle Soul.

Woman of Sorrow invited her into her lodge, claiming she had to "get her ready" to leave the village. She had never seen anybody move so fast. She handed her a buckskin dress with moccasin boots, telling her to put them on, and leave her dress behind. Tempest didn't argue, and did as she was asked.

The dress was beautifully adorned with beads of fine color, and though it squeezed her breasts, and fell too short on her, it was very comfortable. Woman of Sorrow braided her long hair, and announced that she was now ready to travel. After finding Gentle Souls horse, Woman of Sorrow helped her mount him, handed her a pouch of food and a canteen of water, before slapping the horse on the ass. "May the Gods look after you white woman." She spoke into the wind. Tempest held on for dear life, while Black Wing rode into the wind, becoming one with it. This horse was made to run, Tempest thought to herself-just like her. She wondered how long it would take Gentle Soul to realize she was missing from camp.

Chapter Sixteen

Gentle Soul awoke with a start. Something was wrong. He could feel it. He turned to find Little Doe sleeping behind him and looked for Tempest, but Tempest wasn't there. He felt a grave unease come over him, at finding her gone. Without looking, he even knew she was not in the lodge. He got up immediately and ran outside, looking for her. He searched the river to see if she had decided to bathe, but she wasn't there either. He did find her dress on the grassy spot in front of the river. The dress was torn and had spots of blood on it. He went very still, as he thought of the many scenarios that could have happened to her. Finally, he decided to go to his friend, Dancing Eyes.

He was surprised to find Woman of Sorrow with Dancing Eyes so soon. "I'm looking for Tempest. She's gone, and I can't find her anywhere." Dancing Eyes looked back at Woman of Sorrow, but obviously neither knew anything. "I must go find her-she is not well and doesn't know the harsh land, or the troubles that await her. Besides, I found her dress. It was bloodied, lying on the grass in front of the river."

Woman of Sorrow gasped when she saw him hold up the dress, and then she started crying as she spoke to both of them. "I'm so sorry. I didn't know about Dancing Eyes wanting me. I thought...I thought I would be shamed, and left alone, you must believe me!"

Gentle Soul put his hands on Woman of Sorrow and shook her in fear. "What do you know? Tell me now!"

Dancing Eyes looked at Woman of Sorrow. "Tell him if you know anything about this woman. Just as you are now my woman, the white woman holds a special place in Gentle Souls heart..."

Whiskey Woman

"She came here asking for my help to get away...I gave her your horse, food, water and one of my dresses, and put that one by the river so you would think she was gone forever. I am sorry. I was scared..."

"You were jealous!" Gentle Soul snapped at her in fury.

"Now wait a minute! As she has just shared with you, she is my woman now." Dancing Eyes moved in front of Woman of Sorrow to shield her from Gentle Souls accusing stare.

Gentle Soul gritted his teeth. "She better hope I find her then, or I will shun you both from the entire village! And Woman of Sorrow, if any harm comes to her, you better pray to the Gods for mercy, because I won't show you any!"

"Please wait Gentle Soul. I will go with you..." Dancing Eyes offered him.

"No. I go by myself, but I have need of your horse since she has mine. Black Wing is much too strong for her. Stay here and pray. I will not return until I find her. Please talk to your woman Dancing Eyes. I plan on making Tempest my wife when I bring her back and I will not tolerate any of this nonsense again."

Dancing Eyes had not seen his friend so angry since the raid on their village. He would talk to his woman now and straighten this out. He watched his friend Gentle Soul mount his horse and head out to get his woman...Dancing eyes sent up a cry of help to the Gods, and hoped they heard his prayer...

Tempest was getting tired. She knew nothing about horses, but she bet Black Wing was tired too. The horse was crazy, for sure. She didn't know where they were headed. All she knew is the horse could fly. From the moment she mounted him, he had taken off to take her somewhere he had wanted to go. Apparently, he didn't care what she thought about where he was taking her, but she was too tired to try and figure it out. Besides, all she really wanted to do was get away from the one person who she truly cared for-Gentle Soul. She wondered if he had awoken yet to find her gone. She already missed him. What she was doing was for the best though. She already knew Gentle Soul cared for her-she could feel it in her heart.

The wind had picked up considerably since she had left the village. It was a virtual dirt storm out here. Tempest rubbed aggressively at her eyes, but they wouldn't stop burning. She knew she'd have to stop somewhere now. Besides, she was tired and so was Black Wing. She sure wished she had a tent right now. Instead, she would have to make herself cozy in a cave somewhere, if she was lucky enough to find one she could actually get into without too much trouble.

After thirty minutes of searching for the ideal spot, Tempest finally gave up and settled for a sizeable place under the rock of an overhang. It was the closest thing to a roof as she could get, and that was good enough for her. Black wing stood close by and waited patiently. He was a very good horse, Tempest thought.

She would have to rough it for awhile, because she didn't know how to start a fire, she didn't bring a blanket to shield her from the winds, or the dirt flying everywhere, and hell, she didn't have a clue where she was either. Too bad she didn't have a cell phone. She could be out of here in no time. She might have to make the pouch of dried venison jerky Woman of Sorrow packed her last for awhile. She took the pouch and the water pouch and placed them beside her, under the sheltering roof of the rock. After that, she leaned her back up against the rock and sat there and thought about what had happened and what might happen in the future. Tempest nodded off and never heard the footsteps approaching her.

Meanwhile, Gentle Soul followed the tracks Black Wing had made all the way into a dirt storm. He had ridden hell-bent in pursuit of Tempest, and it was paying off now. He noticed the tracks that Black Wing had made and gazed up around the mountain side. There, he saw Black Wing. He dismounted the horse he rode on and began to walk over to where a sleeping Tempest was. He was relieved to find her unharmed and resting.

He stopped, just ten foot away from her, and watched her sleep while sitting up. It both angered him and saddened him to know that she wanted to leave him. He didn't understand the woman at all. Last night she acted like she was happy to be with him. He wondered what had changed her mind that she was willing to risk her life for to get away from him. He knew in his heart, they were meant to be together, but how could he convince her?

Chapter Seventeen

Tempest felt something tickling her face and swatted it. It didn't do her any good, the pesky thing kept tickling her until she came awake and realized she was not dealing with an annoying insect. Gentle Souls face was close to hers when she opened her eyes finally. She instinctively jerked backwards. She looked into his eyes and wished she hadn't. He looked angry to her. "What the hell? You're supposed to be sleeping Gentle Soul..."

"How can I sleep when my woman is gone from my arms?" He looked at her, and she could see the hurt in his eyes too. She didn't want to hurt him, but she knew she must-for his sake later on.

"I'm not your woman Gentle Soul. I think I might've been feverish when I told you that." She noticed his unbelief. "I'm sorry about it, but it is what it is. I don't wish to stay with you any longer-so you can go now..."

"If I go-you go too! You're mine Whiskey."

"Quit saying that Gentle Soul! I am not yours!" she flared her nostrils.

"I see I will have to convince you Whiskey Woman." He said stubbornly.

Tempest crossed her arms and stomped her foot. "You can't make me want you Gentle Soul."

Gentle Soul didn't reply-he just stepped closer, which pushed her back up against the rock, and before she could protest, he zeroed in on her mouth and kissed her. At first he punished her with his kiss, but slowly, as she began to respond, he gentled the pressure and growled deep in his throat. His arms wrapped around her and he held her very close to him-close enough for her to feel the heat of his body. She was intoxicating to all of his senses. When his tongue delved into her mouth, she held onto him dearly. As his mouth made a descending trip to her neck, he heard her mewling like a lost kitten. His hands went into her hair and he wrapped the bulk of it in his hands as he continued kissing her. Her knees buckled under the assault on her senses but he held onto her until he could push her back up against the wall of rock.

"I want to feel your heat Whiskey."

Tempest wanted to make love to him so bad it hurt, but she knew that would only make things worse between them. So she broke away from him.

"I can't do this Gentle Soul. We cannot be together."

"You would deny what I know your body wants?"

Tempest was angry things couldn't be different between them. Gentle Soul would never understand the truth. "No. What I want is to be away from you Gentle Soul."

Gentle Soul bristled at the note of finality in her statement. "I refuse to let you go Whiskey Woman. You are not safe to be away from me. I must know you will be okay. Then, and only then, will I let you leave, if that is still your wish." Gentle Soul backed away from her then, and she was sure she had never seen a man as dejected as he looked right now. It broke her heart for him, but he would never understand why she had to do it, so she didn't bother telling him. Instead, she pulled her dress back onto her thighs and re-did the hair that had come loose. This was no time to be falling into his arms when she knew she couldn't have him. There was no point in both of them getting hurt. After all, this was all because of her, not him. She imagined she had enough already to answer for to the Council, without adding more to her list of bad choices. She didn't want to be responsible for his broken heart too. She would have to keep her distance until she went back to Heaven.

Gentle Soul left her there, while he went in search of pine needles to make them a bed for the night. His heart ached at her words. She had talked foolishly ever since he had met her. So why did he want her so much? Maybe, he thought to himself, just maybe, he cared for her because he felt sorry for anybody who showed such sickness as she did. It was obvious she wasn't well, but deep in his soul he knew it was more than that and it bothered him greatly that she didn't return his feelings. She said she didn't want him to warm her blankets either, but her body said something different. Some things just couldn't be lied about, but he wondered why she had felt the need to. Was she scared of him? He didn't think she was, but why would she try to get away from him? There was something she wasn't telling him, and he planned on finding out one way or another. With his mind made up and his arms full of pine branches, he made his way back to Tempest.

He didn't waste time or words. He simply stated, "I know you're hiding something from me Whiskey, and I want to know what it is now. You refused my touch earlier, but I know your body doesn't lie. Tell me you don't want me Whiskey. Tell me to my face."

"I won't deny it Gentle Soul, but we can't act on it. The Gods don't want us together. Besides, since I am alive now, technically, I'm still married to Steve."

Gentle Soul hung his head in defeat. "It is my fault you are still not well. I should've made someone stay with you until you were better. If I had, you wouldn't be talking this nonsense now." He pulled Tempest down with him, and held her firmly on his lap while he talked to her, and voiced his concerns.

"You're wrong Gentle Soul. I was never sick. I have always told you the truth, but you fail to accept it. How can I convince you that what I say is true?"

Gentle Soul could feel her hurt. "Tell me everything, and then I will decide."

Tempest half turned in his lap to smile at him. "Thank you for giving me a chance to explain."

Gentle Soul listened to the whole story and didn't interrupt once. Now he sat with her still on his lap, and he thought about everything she just told him. *This couldn't be!* He thought rather dejectedly to himself.

When he still said nothing, Tempest felt her hopes die. Still, he did not believe her. "Gentle Soul, I have an idea..."

"I'm sorry Whiskey, but I cannot believe such a story as this one. I can promise you that we'll get you help though."

"I don't want help-I want you to believe me!" she cried. "What would it take for you to believe me Gentle Soul?"

"I would have to meet this Angel, Destiny before I would believe you. I'd have to see her face to face Whiskey."

Tempest lifted her face skyward, and began to talk to the heavens. "Dear Gods of heaven, please hear me as I pray to you right now, and answer my cry. Destiny, I call you forth and ask that you come to me and help me. Please come to me Destiny, please..."

The winds picked up around them, and created another dirt storm. They both squinted their eyes against the dirt swirling around them, and both of them saw a figure in the wind that floated towards them.

Gentle Soul couldn't believe his eyes! Right in front of him stood an angel-Destiny. He fell to the ground when he noticed her floating. She didn't look too happy to be here he noted. None of this affected Tempest though. She was clearly not impressed. Everything she had told him was true after all...My God, Tempest really did go to Heaven! His woman knew an angel!!

"Tempest, the God's won't like you bringing me here just so he could believe you. Besides, this changes nothing. Your fate is still to be back in Heaven after this."

"No. Tell them I refuse. I don't want revenge anymore. All I want is right here, with him. I don't care what Steve does. I'm not going back willingly-they'll have to kill me first."

Destiny shook her head in disapproval. "Tempest please don't anger the Gods. They do have all the power over you, you know. If you don't come back when they send for you, they may very well kill you."

Whiskey Woman

Gentle Soul felt his heart plummet. He spoke up to Destiny. "I will not allow them to kill her. When the time comes, I'll make sure she goes with you."

Tempest whirled on him. "Stay out of this Gentle Soul. It's my choice-not yours!"

"I will not let you risk your life for me Whiskey-no matter how badly I want you to be mine. I only want what is best for you. I have already lost one woman to murder, It won't happen again..."

Chapter Eighteen

Destiny had left nearly twenty minutes earlier, but Tempest remained sullen and unusually quiet. She didn't understand why things were going like they were for her. She was angry at the Gods too. Hadn't she suffered enough already? What about Gentle Soul? Had he not suffered enough as well? She shook her head, as if to clear the thoughts away. Gentle Soul was attending to Black Wing. She rose up and went to him.

"I'm sorry Gentle Soul."

"This is not your fault Whiskey."

"If you don't want anything else to do with me, I would understand..." her voice wobbled.

Gentle Soul turned from Black Wing to pull Tempest into his arms. He rested his chin on her head as she buried her face in his chest. "Hush Whiskey. I still want you. I just have to figure out a way to change the minds of the Gods."

She didn't know why, but she trusted Gentle Soul-she believed in him. She clung tightly to him and wished they could remain like this forever. She didn't care about the rest of the world. It was hard to believe just four weeks ago she was killed, sent to heaven, then back to earth to meet Gentle Soul, and expected to leave him when she was starting to really care for him. It was sudden, for sure, but stranger things had happened. For instance, Steve, whom she had spent ten years with, and thought she could trust him because he was her husband. Her own husband had killed her. Gentle Soul had just met her, but he treated her better than Steve ever had. She wanted to see what Gentle Soul and she could have...just a last chance to know love-if love was possible for her. Her heart was full of regret right now. Would she go back to heaven without ever having been truly loved? She hoped not. She didn't want to live in a heaven where she had to leave love behind. She thought she wanted revenge more than anything when she came back, but no-she wanted love more than anything. Her body trembled with the effort to hold back the cascade of tears she refused to shed.

Gentle Soul offered her the shelter of his embrace. He had no comforting words for her, so he simply held her to him. Tempest wept. Being in his arms was bittersweet, because she hated the thought of one day leaving them-leaving him. How could she convey to Gentle Soul how she felt? Suddenly, nothing else mattered but right now-this moment, and she was going to throw caution to the wind and grab what life and love she could while she was still here-with him. So she lifted her head and kissed him-really kissed him. Gentle Soul could feel the power behind her kiss-even the emotion was clear to him. He held her face in his hands and kissed her back. She needed this, and he needed her. They each explored the others mouth and while he held her face, she let her hands roam freely all over his chest and back. As their kiss deepened, Tempest sucked his lower lip in and gently bit him. Gentle Soul growled and returned the bite. Tempest sighed, and fell against him more heavily, as if she were drugged.

Words weren't necessary, because they both felt the urgency. The only thing they could count on was now-here with each other. Gentle Soul blazed kisses from her jaw, down to her neck, and across her shoulder bone, starting a slow-burning path of fire and need. Tempest arched her back and pushed into his onslaught of kisses. She needed to be closer. Gentle Soul lifted her dress above her head and took it off completely. Her skin was chilled in the open air, and he bent to take a nipple into his mouth, while preparing her other breast for his imminent touch. Tempest was now moaning senselessly. He stepped back to remove his buckskin leggings, never taking his eyes off of her. She stood there, naked, and not ashamed. He took every detail in to remember. She wasn't slender like many other women. She had full breasts, and wide hips that he loved. She looked like a Goddess to him. Her womanhood was bare, without any curls to cover her, and it excited him greatly to be able to see her natural loveliness without anything to block it. "My God Whiskey, you steal the very air in my body!"

His praise fulfilled her. He did nothing less than worship her with his eyes, mouth, and hands. Tempest stepped back and had her fill of gazing at him from head to toe. "You are absolutely beyond beautiful Gentle Soul." Her praise humbled him. She knelt before him and took his hardened, shaft into one hand, while gently kissing his sack. The pleasure was almost too much to bear. She gently stroked his shaft, and then stopped to lick him, and finally take him into her mouth. He knew it wouldn't last if she kept doing that, so he stepped back and reached down to pull her to her feet.

Once she was on her feet again, Gentle Soul then knelt before her and delved into her wet center with his tongue. He licked her as gentle as a butterfly's wings, and the more gentle he was, the hotter she got. She tried to break away to touch him, but he held her still and continued his onslaught of pleasuring her. His licking picked up rapidly, until she was moaning his name, and shaking. He finally drove two fingers into her wetness and moved them rapidly, and deeply. Tempest could feel everything closing in on her, and she thought for sure she'd die from pleasure. Finally, with back arched, she threw back her mane of hair and cried his name aloud.

Gentle Soul could feel her wetness increase as she also became more vocal. He wanted desperately to drive himself into her moist hot center, but not before she was ready for him. Only after he took her over the edge did he stop to push her back against the rock wall, and lift one leg up to hook over one strong arm before he found her opening, and with one thrust pushed himself deeply inside her, to fill her completely. Again, he growled, but louder this time. When he heard her breath catch, he drove into her quite madly, and her cries of pleasure were almost his undoing. He repositioned himself and with her back still against the rock wall, he lifted her up and entered her again. She was spread as far as she could be, and each stroke teased her g-spot. She couldn't take it any longer. "Gentle Soul, I want you to thrust deeper and harder, please…." Gentle Soul drove into her wetness again and again, utterly pounding her, until she let out a screaming of his name and went over the edge in waves upon waves of pleasure. Gentle Soul felt her convulse around his bulging shaft and he rode her like a wild animal until he too went over the edge and planted his seed deep within her. He said her name aloud, again and again, until he was finally sated.

Whiskey Woman

Gentle Soul dressed and went to gather pine needle branches to make them a bed. Tempest watched him as he gathered everything for a bed, as well as a fire. She had a smile on her face, and she couldn't be happier. She silently thanked the Gods for at least letting her have this much.

After making them a bed and starting a fire, Gentle Soul patted a place beside him for Tempest to occupy. When she came and lay down, he wrapped her as close as he could get in his arms, and kissed her cheeks, her lips, and her forehead. "We will find a way to stay together Whiskey Woman…"

Tempest snuggled closer. "I pray we do Gentle Soul, because I don't want to be without you."

They made love until they both were exhausted and happily so.

Chapter Nineteen

Steve was enjoying time spent with Brandi. She had agreed to date him now that enough time had passed. They had really connected in the last few weeks and Steve couldn't be happier. Whenever his conscience began to bother him, all he had to think about was spending time in a prison somewhere. He would rather die than go to prison.

It turned out that Brandi was a "good" girl-much to his disappointment. Obviously, he'd just have to step up his game with her. Girls like Brandi were rare, so he knew he'd have to have her. She challenged him, to a whole new level of the way he operated with women before her. He wasn't a quitter though. He would take her to his bed, and soon, he purposed within himself. He always got what he wanted, and this time would not be any different. Besides, she should be grateful he had chosen her. He didn't know of anyone else knocking down her door to go out. After all, she wasn't a beautiful woman. She should be thrilled he was taking time for her "too good" ass!

He looked at himself in the bathroom mirror. His blonde hair now held patches of grey in it, and his blue eyes had dimmed over the years in their color. However, he wasn't worried. Many women would be glad to be with him. Especially now that he had come into money, thanks to Tempests' death.

Just thinking of Tempest made him sick to his stomach. He didn't miss her big mouth running all the time, or the way she stood up to him in an argument. She was too bossy for his taste. He liked a woman who was quiet and who submitted to him. Tempest was a hell- cat... for all her cared, he hoped she was in hell right now. How dare she try to leave him!

He glanced at the paperwork on his desk. He made a mental note to ask for Brandi's help. She had helped him numerous times before, now shouldn't be any different. All he had to do was turn on his charm-she couldn't deny him anything. Besides, he had better things to do-more important things, like buying Brandi some lingerie. But first, he had to clean up his computer from the porn he watched almost daily now. He laughed to himself. Brandi would be horrified if she knew he watched porn. She was a good Christian woman, with plenty of morals to go around, but she wouldn't be for long if he had his way, and he always got his way in the end...something Tempest had found out too late.

He often thought about that night and every time he did, he was amazed at how brave he had been to do what he did. Tempest had grated on his very last nerve for the last time. It was a shame he had to send her to hell with her pretty face disfigured from the guns blast. Who was he kidding? He didn't regret a damn thing-except maybe doing it a lot sooner than he had.

His eyes latched onto a picture still on his desk of her. He had forgotten about it being there. He had put it there right after the funeral. Every time someone came into his office, they were filled with compassion to the grieving widower. But, it had served its purpose now. So he picked it up, and threw it into the waste basket.

"Goodbye forever Tempest Hawthorne. May you rest in hell forever and your money grant me everything I ever desired. I do hope you can hear me dear. By the way, I'm going to have the life you always denied me. I'm going to start with your friend Brandi." He laughed bitterly.

Chapter Twenty

Gentle Soul woke up with Tempest in his arms. He lay there, in the early morning light and absorbed everything in his surroundings with great pleasure. He enjoyed the sounds of nature, and he couldn't think of anyone better to share it with. He was still amazed by the woman sleeping beside him. She was everything he had prayed for in a mate, and he refused to let her go without a fight. Even if he had to fight Gods-he wasn't letting her go.

Now he knew why she had left him. She cared too much to see him hurt. It took guts to do what she did, and though he didn't agree with her decision, he did respect her for it. But she wasn't going to leave him again. He would do everything in his power to make her want to stay more than leave for his sake out of fear.

He thought about Silent Speaks, and how much he had loved her. He never thought it possible to love a woman again, but he did. In fact, he loved Tempest with a passion he never knew existed until now. He knew in his heart, Silent Speaks would want him to move on, so he silently asked for her blessings as well as help in the heavens to keep Tempest with him always.

Tempest stirred beside Gentle Soul, and he watched her come awake slowly. As soon as she opened her eyes, she had a satisfied smile on her face for him. Her hair lay all around her in a halo effect, and he knew he was waking up to the most beautiful angel heaven had ever seen, a real-life earth-angel, and she was all his.

He turned toward her, facing her, so he could look into her golden eyes. "Good morning Whiskey; How did you sleep?"

Tempest stretched like a kitten. "I slept wonderfully. How did you sleep?"

He could see her eyes twinkling with mischief. So, he quickly covered her body with his own and playfully held her down. Tempest giggled like a school child, in delight. She absolutely glowed this morning, and he wondered if their lovemaking had done that for her. If so, he would have to oblige her more often. He enjoyed hearing her laugh, and watching her play with him without reserve. She half-heartedly wiggled beneath his hold and it only excited him. He knew she knew exactly what she was doing to him right now, but she had no guilt, and no shame. "Woman, you wiggle beneath me and make my body like a young rutting buck in season. Stop it now." He chastised her with no real effort.

Tempest wasn't wiggling long. Gentle Soul reached down to cup her sex in his hand and she immediately went still. He laughed at her sudden change. He whispered his most villainess voice into her ear. "Have you ever been captured by an Indian before, Miss?" he breathed into her ear softly and hotly. She shuddered and his fingers delved into her heat. She was already slick from wanting him. The knowledge made him painfully hard.

"No. I have not ever been captured by an Indian. Would you like to be the first?" she said cheekily.

Gentle Soul's eyes grew darker at once. "I want to be your first and last." He growled at her, while nudging her knees apart in a hurried motion.

Tempest arose to the challenge in his voice. "Well then, I suggest you learn how to keep me Indian..." Gentle Soul plunged into her heat and sank deeply into her. Tempest raised each leg and pushed upward to reach his thrusts. "Oh yes Gentle Soul..." she said into his mouth, while she found his tongue and danced with it. Her hands roamed all over the front of his chest and his arms as he continued his slow pace with her. She needed more-now. "More...give me more-faster Gentle Soul..." She begged him. Gentle Soul could hear the urgency in her voice, and felt the evidence of passion in her trembling body. He couldn't hold back any longer. He bent down to kiss her as he drove into her, and as she started to writhe in pleasure, he took her faster and faster, until they both reached their plateau.

Gentle Soul lay beside her and pulled her into his arms again, and she rested her head on his shoulder. Neither one of them spoke-they didn't have to. They simply lay there- both content to hold one another as they each got lost in their own thoughts.

Gentle Soul had never been scared of anything, until now. He didn't want to lose Tempest to the Gods. He had no idea of how he could change their minds, or keep her hidden away from them should they try to come after her.

Tempest was thinking the same thing. She didn't want to go back to heaven anymore than he wanted her to leave him, but she saw no real hope of getting away from it. There was no use fighting against the Gods. She would never win. She knew all she could do now was pray, and enjoy the time she still had with Gentle Soul and Little Doe.

She turned her head to look at him closely. He was every bit a proud warrior, and she felt blessed to have met him. As beautiful as he was, no stranger would believe he was soft-hearted too. She supposed that was a good thing though-especially living in this era in life. She ran her fingertips all over his face, as if to memorize every feature-every detail. Her heart fluttered when she touched his lips, and he stilled her searching fingers with his hand, and whispered, "I love you Whiskey."

Tempest felt her heart swell with her own emotions. "Gentle Soul, I think I have always loved you-even before I met you." They both held onto each other for a little while longer...

Heaven

Destiny cried. It was obvious that Gentle Soul and Tempest loved each other. It broke Destiny's heart to know they couldn't be together for eternity. She wished there was something she could say to the Gods to change their minds, but she didn't have a clue...

Chapter Twenty-One

Gentle Soul and Tempest started back to the village on Black Wing. Tempest sat as close as she could to him and wrapped her arms around him. She inhaled his scent. He smelled like nature. She couldn't think of a time where she had been any happier than she was right now with the man she loved so dearly. For the first time she could remember, she prayed a prayer of thanks to the God of Love.

Gentle Soul could feel his woman's happiness without looking at her. This brought him great pleasure. He knew now, just how special she was. After seeing the angel appear he finally understood everything Tempest had told him-except one...*Why would a man who claimed to love his wife kill her?* The man had better hope Gentle Soul never met him, because he would make the man's death as painful as he could after what he did to Tempest. Clearly the man was not right in the head. He couldn't see anyone hating Tempest that badly. She even stepped in and fought for Little Doe. Gentle Soul's heart filled with pride. He didn't know of any other female who would have done what she did. Yes-she was strong in heart and passion.

They rode for two hours until he came to the river that also ran aside his village. The village was another hour ahead, but he dismounted and helped Tempest down too. He let Black Wing graze after leading her to the water.

Tempest stretched her long legs and took time to enjoy the view. It was a calm, warm day. She could hear nature all around them, and it sounded as peaceful as she felt. The river flowed gently and she delighted in seeing the many deer come to drink from it. She loved it here. It was unseasonably warm today, and she was grateful that it was. She thought about the last time she had been at a river.

Steve had taken her to the river in her hometown in Prestonsburg, Ky. to propose to her. She was young and naïve then. She remembered how excited she was back then, and realized now how foolish it had all been...the day, the reason...the man. *Why couldn't she see what he really was? Why did he marry her if he didn't even love her? Or did he?* If there was one thing she could ask him, it would be "why"? No matter how much she loved Gentle Soul, they couldn't be married until she was divorced, and Steve didn't even know she was alive. How in the world would he find out? She wondered if The Gods would give her the chance to see him again. Most likely, they would have to, if they wanted her to divorce him. As things stood, the bastard thought she was dead, and was probably spending all her money right now.

Gentle Soul stole her attention by coming up behind her to wrap his strong arms around her. "I love you Whiskey Woman." He whispered near her ear, while hugging her tightly. She could never get tired of him saying those words to her, and she believed he was sincere.

"Gentle Soul, how will I get a divorce with Steve living in another state and time?"

Gentle Soul thought about her question. "I do not have the answers right now Whiskey, but do not worry. The Gods will make a way. I pray it will be soon, because you stay in my dreams, whether I am sleeping or awake. I want you to be rid of this white man who is so evil, so we can share many moons together, and I only want to share my blanket with you to warm me and give me children."

Tempest didn't balk at the idea of having Gentle Soul's child. In fact, she smiled at the thought of carrying his baby, and it made her content to think about it. She wondered about Little Doe. She was glad they would be returning back to the village after resting a bit. She missed Little Doe and Loving Heart. She could almost be content as she looked forward to a future with Gentle Soul and Little Doe in it, but she wouldn't allow herself to be in denial when she knew she couldn't stay. Still, Gentle Soul would not give up on the idea. So, she would have to content herself in living for the moments and time they could share now, until the God's sent for her.

"What is your heart saying to you Whiskey Woman?"

Tempest forced a smile for Gentle Soul. "My heart is happier than it's ever been my love."

Gentle Soul smiled his pleasure and pride. "My heart swells with great love for you Whiskey." He turned her around to face him. "I never thought I would feel for another woman after Silent Speaks was murdered. The God's have blessed me by bringing you to me, and I will find a way to keep you. We are meant to be, like the sun is meant to come out and the moon." He raised one hand to touch her cheek as he spoke. "I will find this Steve and you will get your divorce, if it's the last thing I do. I make you this promise with a clear heart."

Tempest felt tears spike her lashes. Gentle Soul put his strong arms around her and she rose up on tip-toe to kiss him. "Gentle Soul, you have made me happier than I've been in a long time. I don't want a life without you in it. I would rather die than be without you."

Gentle Soul stood back to look at her face as he talked. "No more foolish talk about death. All will be well my woman. Now come-we must gather our things and ride home now."

Heaven

Destiny had a meeting with the Council. She stood in the throne room patiently waiting for one of them to talk. She hoped The Gods had changed their minds about Tempest and Gentle Soul because both were quickly growing on her.

The God of Love spoke up first. "I done well with Tempest and Gentle Soul, did I not?"

Destiny agreed. "Yes, they both seem to truly love each other. This is the first time Tempest has experienced real love, and they are both very happy. Gentle Soul has loved before, but it was never a love this deep, and he is happy too."

The God of Love smiled at such praise. The God of Life then spoke. "I saved Tempest from death at the medicine woman's hands. I am pleased she is so happy."

"Yes God of Life, she is very thankful for that."

The God of Love, and The God of Life both waited on The God of Judgment to say something.

"Judgment must come to Tempest's husband for killing her. Then we will make more decisions."

Chapter Twenty-Two

Steve was going through Tempest's jewelry box. He was picking through her jewelry when he found a pair of diamond earrings that he snatched up. Today was Brandi's birthday, and he wanted to get her something nice. What better present than diamonds? It wasn't like Tempest was going to miss them. He inspected them again, and he was pleased that they would do very nicely. Brandi would love them, and she would think he went out of his way for her gift, but the truth was, he never bought gifts for his wife-never had. Brandi would never know they weren't new after he took them to the jeweler to be cleaned and set in a new box. He slipped them in his pocket for later.

He glanced around their bedroom. Everything looked the same as it had when Tempest was here with him, but he felt an uneasy feeling come over him. Goosebumps rose up the back of his neck and he grabbed the earrings and left the bedroom. He knew it was all in his head but he almost felt like there was someone else in the bedroom with him-which was so ridiculous he laughed to himself. It wasn't conceivable that anybody was there, let alone a ghost…

Destiny disturbed the air around the bedroom Steve was in. She couldn't help it. He was an evil, greedy man, and a murderer. She didn't like him one bit. She thought about how bad Tempest looked when she had come to Heaven. It was hard to believe any husband could kill his wife with such blatant disregard or be as void of feeling as he was. She hoped the Gods were watching him-especially the God of Judgment. She prayed his judgment would come soon.

She was disgusted that Steve planned on giving Brandi his dead wife's jewelry. The man's heart was black and utterly cold. For a brief moment, Destiny wondered why Tempest had stayed with him. Tempest was not only lovely to look at, but she had a beautiful soul and a heart as loving as a child's. She couldn't stand to watch this man keep doing bad things. She sent a prayer up in hopes the God's would do something soon, before another woman got hurt. She needed to visit Tempest again.

She left the bedroom to follow Steve. She found him in the entryway to their home. He laid the earrings down to put on his shoes and Destiny used her energy to pick them up and transport them back to Tempest's jewelry box in the bedroom.

Once Steve had his shoes on, he grabbed his keys and swept his hand to grab the earrings, but his hand never touched them. He looked up then to grab them once more but they were gone. Again, he felt goose bumps, but he was getting frustrated now. "What the hell...?"

He checked his watch. He was running late. He took the stairs two at a time up to the bedroom. After he was inside, he went to the jewelry box-again. The earrings were there once more. Steve shook his head in confusion. As he went to grab the earrings again, he felt something brush his arm and he dropped them on the floor. In an angry burst, he bent and retrieved them once more. This time he held a death grip on them. "Tempest, if that's you trying to scare me, go to hell where you belong!"

Chapter Twenty-Three

Tempest and Gentle Soul had been back for over a week. Tempest was learning how to do everything an Indian woman did for her husband, and though Gentle Soul was not her husband, it made her feel good to take part in what the other women did here. Her days seemed shorter as she worked side by side with other women in the village, and she had even made new friends.

One day when she was bathing at the river, Woman of Sorrow approached her hesitantly. She was washing her hair beside Loving Heart when she heard Woman of Sorrow speak to her.

"*Mah-tao-yo* Whiskey Woman-make room for me." For the first time, Tempest saw her giggle and all her wariness fled then. It was good. Tempest moved to make room for her and they bathed in smiles. When Little Doe came out to bathe with her they all played with her. Little Doe shrieked as each woman pretended to catch her. Tempest felt a strong pull at heart watching Little Doe with these women. Little Doe belonged here. Tempest could not take her with her whenever the Gods came to get her. *How could she ever leave here without her or Gentle Soul?*

"What brings sadness to you Whiskey Woman? Are you not happy here among the people? Do you miss your wooden walls?"

Tempest looked carefully into Woman of Sorrow's eyes. She found sincerity where she thought great malice would be. "It is nothing Woman of Sorrow." She lied.

"Don't be *boisa*-crazy. I can see the sadness in the water that springs from your eyes."

Tempest swallowed hard, trying hard not to burst into more tears in front of the women. "You must think of me as a weak *white eyes*."

Woman of Sorrow shook her head vigorously. "I have seen your great strength. You acted as the people would over Little Doe, and you have made Gentle Soul happy again. We not get a good start before, but we start over, heh?" She smiled hopefully at Tempest, and Tempest smiled back.

"Yes. A new start is good." She agreed.

"I have good enough man now. Dancing Eyes has claimed me before the central fire, to be his wife. I was wrong about many things. Gentle Soul makes eyes for only you. It is good, heh?"

Tempest wished she could tell Woman of Sorrow her fears, but she knew she could not. She smiled at Woman of Sorrow. "Yes. It is good."

"Gentle Soul was plenty sad when my sister died. I took care of him and he took care of me after the *Comanchero* raped and murdered her in front of Gentle Soul. I thought I was meant to be his woman in place of my sister. That is how it is done here, but then he met you and he was right-I was jealous. I had gotten used to having his strong arm to protect me and provide for me, and I thought I loved him, but now that Dancing Eyes has claimed me, I know how wrong I was. I love Gentle Soul as a brother, but I am deep in love with Dancing Eyes."

"I'm happy for you both, and I'm so sorry you lost your sister in such a bad way Woman of Sorrow."

Tempest went back to Gentle Soul's lodge and started a fire to prepare supper. She thought about what Woman of Sorrow had shared with her, and it made her sad. She wondered if Gentle Soul thought about his dead wife. If he did, he done it in private, away from her. *Did he love Silent Speaks more than he loved her?* It was silly to even wonder about such things, seeing as how the woman was dead. She was pathetic-jealous over a dead woman. Pfft!

Gentle Soul lifted the flap to the entryway and came in holding Little Doe on his broad shoulders. The girl was laughing loudly with pleasure at Gentle Soul growling at her playfully. While still holding Little Doe on his shoulders, he came up to Tempest and kissed her openly in front of the child. Though it pleased Tempest, she scolded him in mock anger. All three of them laughed. Gentle Soul let Little Doe down unto the pallet of buffalo furs and tickled her tiny belly. Tempest watched them play, and she knew she had hopelessly fallen in love with Gentle Soul. His natural way of loving her and Little Doe touched her more than any gift she had ever received before.

"Sit down you two. I have supper ready." As they obeyed her, she ladled them both out some venison stew with dried berries for dessert. They ate in a comfortable silence. Afterwards, Gentle Soul told them a story in front of the fire. Tempest was just as interested in the story as Little Doe was, and they both listened to Gentle Soul weave a beautiful story about a warrior falling in love with a white eyes. Little Doe fell asleep before the end, but Tempest was mesmerized by it, and wanted to hear how it ended. Suddenly, Gentle Soul stopped the story.

"Why did you stop?" she asked him.

"In time, you will know the end of this story *mah-tao-yo.*" He smiled, teasing her curiosity.

"But I want to know how it ends with the Indian Chief and his white eyes captive."

Gentle Soul smiled a mischievous smile at her. "It ends how we make it end Whiskey Woman. Tell me how you wish it to end white eyes."

Tempest now knew why he didn't tell her the end of it. The story was about her and him, which was why it fascinated her so much. "I want it to end with them getting to spend the rest of their lives together-for always Gentle Soul."

"Then we must make the story end in that way mah-tao-yo."

"What does that mean, that word?"

"My little one."

Tempest smiled. "I like that."

Gentle Soul picked Little Doe up and laid her on her own furs, a few feet from theirs, before joining Tempest under his own buffalo robes.

Tempest felt a little nervous wondering if Gentle Soul would try to make love to her with Little Doe beside them, but she need not to have worried.

Gentle Soul pulled her close to him and simply kissed her head, as he stroked her hair, and they slept peacefully, all three of them.

Chapter Twenty-Four

Brandi had loved the diamond earrings Steve gave her. Her face lit up with excitement when he presented them to her. She put them on right away. They enjoyed a nice dinner and Steve asked her back to his place. Brandi came willingly.

"Grab a seat in the living room while I fix us a drink."

Instead, Brandi walked around the living room to look at the pictures above the fireplace. One of those pictures were of Tempest with a book in her hand, smiling. "She looks so happy here Steve…"

Steve handed her the drink he'd made for her and scowled at the picture. "Yes, I suppose so, writing came first for Tempest. She loved it more than she loved me." He scowled.

Brandi turned questioning eyes to him. "What does that mean Steve?"

Steve tried to shrug it off. "Nothing. It means absolutely nothing sweetheart. Tempest is gone now, and there's only you and me now. You're all I want. You make me happy; come here." He held his arms out welcomingly to her and she came into them and hugged him close. Steve held her tight as he thought about taking her to bed. He bent his head down and kissed her. Brandi kissed him back shyly, but when his hands started to wander to her breasts, she backed away, denying him access.

"What are you trying to do Steve?"

Steve didn't appreciate having to defend himself to a mere woman. "I want to take you to bed Brandi. I thought you'd be ready now."

"I'm sorry Steve, but I can't just go to bed with you. I'm saving myself for my future husband."

"Brandi come on...it's *me*." He whined.

Brandi backed away from his embrace. "I'm sorry Steve, but we can't do this. I thought you respected me enough to wait..." There was a question in her voice.

Steve pursed his lips and ran a weary hand through his hair. He grit his teeth. "Of course I respect you. Brandi, I love you. Don't you want to make love with the man who loves you?"

"You love me?"

He could hear the disbelief in her question. He laughed. "Of course I do. How could I not? You're a very beautiful woman with a heart of gold. Any man would be proud to call you his."

Brandi beamed smile at him. "Thank you Steve. I don't know what to say..."

"How about you love me too and you want to make love now...?"

"I don't know how I feel about you Steve. Tempest hasn't even been dead for long..."

Steve raised his voice impatiently. "Who cares how long she's been dead?? What about me, damn it? What about my needs, huh?"

Brandi could feel the anger in him, and she backed away slowly. "I must go now Steve."

Steve watched Brandi leave and he balled up his fists. He knew he could've stopped her, but it wasn't the right time for that-no, he had to be patient for awhile longer. Tomorrow he would send her roses and apologize for his unseemly behavior, but for tonight, he was pissed off. He walked over to the fireplace and grabbed the picture Brandi was looking at of Tempest and tossed it into the burning fireplace. It made him feel somewhat better, so he decided to collect all the pictures of Tempest and throw them all in the fire. He climbed the stairs two at a time to their bedroom and grabbed those too.

When he came back down with all her pictures, he gasped at what he saw. The picture he had thrown into the fire was sitting on the fireplace, and not one end of it had burned. He felt the hairs on his neck raise. "What the hell?"

Like before, he felt the air stir around him, but instead of being scared he was livid with anger now.

"I know somebody's here. You better come out now before I call the police and have you locked up..."

Incredulously, he faintly heard what sounded like a woman's giggle. "I mean it! Come out now or I will find you and hurt you!"

This time the giggling was much louder and he began pitching the pictures into the fire with a lot of force. Again, the air around him swirled and wrapped around him like a cocoon almost. He took in a shaky breath and stood there mesmerized at what he saw next. Every single picture came flying out of the fireplace with great force and landed on the walls behind him, with no nail to hold them up. Steve felt his knees wobble and strain to hold him up.

"Who the hell's there, damn you?" He shouted.

Angrily, he gathered all the pictures up and threw them into the fire with such force, they all shattered their glass. With a victorious grin he watched them all disappear in the flames and smoke.

"Is that you Tempest? Are you trying to *haunt* me now? You don't scare me!"

This time he heard nothing. He turned to walk out of the room and spotted all the pictures on the walls again. He fainted.

Destiny laughed aloud now. She couldn't stand Steve. The man was nothing but trouble. She wanted to move him somewhere else-anywhere else that he wouldn't hurt anybody else, but she knew she'd have to get permission first from the Gods.

So, for now, she must be content on just watching him and of course, playing with his head as much as possible. If Tempest couldn't have the one thing she wanted mostly in her life-love, then why should he be free to enjoy create more trouble and take pleasure in using someone else again? Destiny wondered for the first time if Tempest's attitude had grown on her and she smiled.

Chapter Twenty-Five

Willow missed her daughter, Little Doe. Gentle Soul would not permit her to even visit Little Doe. It was all because of the white woman. She hated Tempest with all her might. The whole village had turned their backs from facing her after that woman dared to accuse her of beating her own child.

Willow had watched them from a distance. Little Doe had taken right up with the white woman, and Willow seethed with anger. She would have to punish Little Doe for this and the white woman too. The whole village had accepted the white woman as one of their own-it was disgusting. Day after day, she watched as each one of them brought food, blankets and gifts to Gentle Soul's lodge. They weren't even married!

Little Doe cared for the white woman-she could see it clearly as the child held her hand whenever they went out from the lodge, and she even betrayed her own *pia*-mother, by calling the white woman her *pia*.

That morning, she watched all three of them leave the lodge to go down to the river. She decided to sneak behind the lodge and lay in wait there. She knew she must be patient. There would come a time when she could catch them all off guard...

Gentle Soul had announced earlier this morning to take them all down to the river to play on the grass nearby. Little Doe was so excited, and that made it all worth it, Tempest thought to herself. She packed them some beef jerky and dried fruit. Little Doe was lifted up to rest atop Gentle Soul's broad shoulders and the three of them walked down to the river.

Gentle Soul made crude fishing poles for Little Doe and Tempest, and Tempest surprised him by showing Little Doe how to fish. His face smiled as big as his heart did with pride. His woman surprised him every day it seemed. He wanted to make Tempest his wife, but he still had to find

Steve to do that. He didn't think the divorce was necessary, but it was for Tempest. So, he had no other choice but to find the man and get it done, but where should he look? Obviously he wouldn't be here anywhere, since this was back in time. He would try talking to the angel himself, maybe she could help them. In the meantime, he was going to enjoy all the time he had with Tempest.

He watched her fish with Little Doe and he laughed at Little Doe when she caught a fish and brought it in on the bank. The fish flopped wildly and Little Doe squealed excitedly, while Tempest laughed and jumped around. "*Mah-tao-yo, hina-unu-yaaka?*" Tempest asked Little Doe. Gentle Heart swelled with pride when he heard her speak his language. She had just asked Little Doe, "Little one, what do you have in your hand?"

He walked over to them and took the fish and placed it in a crude bucket he had made, while patting Little Doe's head and kissing Tempest quickly. She was flushed with pride, and he was glad to see it. "My woman is great fisherman, heh?" he smiled at her.

"No. Your woman is the bomb!" she laughed.

"The bomb?"

"It means I'm the best." She could tell he thought she was too. She smiled playfully at him.

Willow stood at the backside of Gentle Soul's lodge, waiting for the three of them to return. It angered her to hear Little Doe giggling loudly with Tempest. She would stop that as soon as she had the right opportunity.

Two hours later, all three of them came back to the lodge, and she could hear them talking. She rest her back against the lodges wall and slid down to a sitting position as she listened and waited.

Gentle Soul carried a sleepy Little Doe in and laid her down on her furs, while Tempest took the bucket of fish and started to clean them. Soon, he would smell the scent of fish fill the lodge. It was a good day. He went to sit beside the fireplace and watch Tempest work. She was beautiful-standing there with fish guts all over her hands. He was happy. All they needed now was to find Steve and get this divorce Tempest told him about.

Tempest worked in silence, but she wondered what Gentle Soul was thinking about. It was clear to see that he was in a good mood today, and he was very happy. She was too. She just wished they could find Steve so she could get her divorce.

Tempest finished with cleaning the fish and prepared them to be cooked. "Gentle Soul, how will we ever find Steve? Is it even possible?"

"I don't know yet. I'm thinking on it. All is well, no? We are happy, yes?"

Tempest smiled. "Yes. We are happy, but I must get the divorce before I can marry you."

Gentle Soul got up and come to stand behind Tempest. He nuzzled her neck as he spoke. "So you will marry me, heh?"

"Yes. I will marry you, as soon as I get a divorce from Steve."

"You love me great big, heh?"

"I love you bigger than great big." She giggled as he traced the shell of her ear with his tongue. Tempest shivered in excitement.

"Whiskey, I want to announce that you have agreed to become my wife at the central fire tonight."

"Shouldn't we wait until I get my divorce Gentle Soul?"

"We both know what we want. Why not announce it to the people?"

"What would the people think, if they knew I was already married?"

"They wouldn't like it, but they don't know, so I will announce it tonight."

"I just hope nobody finds out Gentle Soul. It would not look good on either of us, but you especially, since you're the chief of your people."

"Do not worry so much. My people already love you Whiskey."

Willow smiled like a fox. *So Tempest was married, huh? How would the people feel about that, she wondered? She would soon find out...*

Woman of Sorrow came by the lodge to visit while Gentle Soul had things to take care of. In her hands she held a beautiful dress she had made for Tempest, as well as a pair of ornately stitched moccasins for her feet. Tempest held the dress up for inspection. The dress was made from deer fur and it had beautiful shells and other bead work on it. Tempest was overwhelmed at such a gift. "Oh Woman of Sorrow, this is absolutely beautiful! How can I ever thank you?"

"I'm glad you are pleased Whiskey Woman. It is I that should thank you for bringing the heart back of our chief. Today is a good day, no?"

Tempest laughed with tears in her eyes. "Yes. Today is very good!" She surprised Woman of Sorrow by hugging her tightly.

"I will take Little Doe now to my lodge, and keep her for tonight."

Tempest watched Little Doe clap her tiny hands in approval, but for some reason, she felt a little uneasy. She knew it was silly, because Woman of Sorrow would never hurt the child, but something made her feel uneasy about the night ahead of them all.

"Whiskey Woman, you frown like sad pup. What's wrong?"

Tempest shook her head and laughed. "Look over me Woman of Sorrow. I think it's just bad nerves. Don't worry-I'll be okay. I promise."

Little Doe hugged her before launching herself into Woman of Sorrows arms. "Bye *Pia. Kamakutu-nu...*"

Tempest raised an eyebrow.

"It means mother, and I love you." Woman of Sorrow explained.

"Little Doe, kamakutu-nu." She spoke to the child as she kissed her cheek then watched them disappear from the lodge.

Tempest gathered soap and perfume water to go get a bath in the river. For the first time since she'd arrived here, she started to feel hopeful that everything really would work out. She whispered heartfelt thank you to the God's...

Gentle Soul had spent his time with Dancing Eyes, and told him of all that Tempest had shared with him, as well as meeting the angel, Destiny. Dancing Eyes shared his pipe with Gentle Soul and listened intently as he heard the story unfold. He had heard that people see visions before, but this was a miracle. "Your woman speaks with angels Gentle Soul. It is a good thing for our people that she does. She will bring only good luck to our people, but you must find a way to get this divorce for her, or the people will not accept her."

He only voiced what Gentle Soul had already thought. He must find a way to release her from this marriage, and soon. He sighed heavily at the daunting task ahead of him. "Tell me brother, how do I find the man from her future to get this divorce?"

"If the Gods sent her here, then only the Gods can do it. Ask them to do it."

Gentle Soul stood and hugged his best friend, whom he considered like as unto a brother.

Chapter Twenty-Six

Every Comanche warrior and his wife and children had gathered together to hear what their chief wanted to tell them that night. All of them were eager to hear the good news, and most already suspected it would be an announcement of his upcoming desire to marry Whiskey Woman. Many of the women had brought prepared food while some others brought many blankets and made eating utensils to present to the couple.

Nobody paid any attention to Willow being there. It was as if she was invisible to them. It angered her greatly. She latched eyes onto Tempest and shook with her rage. Tempest stood there in front of all the people looking like a Goddess, while holding *her* baby girl and looking up adoringly into Gentle Souls face. Gentle Soul lifted his left arm to silence the people as he began his speech to them.

"My people, as you all know, I have not been the same since losing my wife to the Comanchero's a few years ago. My heart was made heavy by her death. I will not speak her name as that is bad, no? But I asked for you all to gather tonight to hear my great news." The people cheered as he pulled Tempest closer to his side and smiled at her with all his love in his eyes for all to see.

"Since I met this woman I have never felt such joy in my heart. She has made it possible for me to love again, when I thought I could not. My people, I hope you will make friends with her if you haven't already, because it is my promise to you and to her that because I love her, I will marry her." The people cheered their approval for a few minutes, before they once again become silent to hear what their chief would say next.

"My woman has taken to Little Doe, and as you all must know, it was because of her that we now have a daughter of the people-Little Doe. Little Doe loves Tempest and she is doing very well..."

"She stole my daughter!" Willow shouted above the crowd.

"Please take her to her lodge Dancing Eyes." Gentle Soul asked his friend.

"No. I'm not going anywhere until I tell the truth! Your woman fools the people and so do you Gentle Soul! She already has a husband, but now she carries lies to our people, and you let her, do you not?" she taunted with venom.

The people became eerily silent at this last remark. Somebody asked, "Is this true Gentle Soul? Is she already married?"

Gentle Soul held Tempest shaky gaze with his own filled with regret. "It is true, but we are finding a way to get her divorce."

This did not sit well with his people at all. "How could you lie to us?"

"Go home white eyes…" some chanted cruelly at Tempest. The crowd was now angry with Tempest and Gentle Soul. Woman of Sorrow stepped forward.

"You all would forget so easily how this woman saved a child of our people? Or how our chief has provided for us all in the great hunt? How he has led us in victory against those who seek to hurt us?" she stood beside the two of them. "I will stand behind our chief and his woman, no matter what." Will you?" Many of the people bowed their heads in shame. She was right. Their loyalty returned, one by one, as they all took turns shaking their chief's hand and presenting gifts to them both. Willow couldn't believe the people would turn back so easily. She shouldn't be surprised though, it was these same people who took her daughter away from her because of a *tosi tovo*. She sneered her contempt for Tempest as she declined shaking their hands or offering gifts. She went back to her lodge to sulk.

Gentle Soul was both relieved and proud of his people. The situation tonight could have gone very badly had it not been for Woman of Sorrow. The people were still celebrating into the night over the good news, but he and Tempest were back at the lodge, and his woman lay naked under his buffalo furs-waiting on him to join her with a smile.

Tempest beckoned Gentle Soul with her pleading eyes to join her. Words weren't necessary between them right now. Gentle Soul undressed and moved under the furs with her, taking her into his arms and nuzzling her neck. Tempest giggled and shivered in anticipation. She adored this man. She was head over heels in love with an Indian. For the first time since her arrival here, she was thankful the Gods had sent her here. Gentle Soul sought her mouth and she kissed him with her heart in it. How could she ever survive away from his love? She didn't want to think about it right now. No-for now, she just wanted to feel his hands lightly running up and down her body. Tonight was about them. She blocked out everything else but Gentle Soul.

Gentle Soul knew Tempest was worried, but he also knew when she stopped thinking and focused only on his touch. He lifted the cover back and eyed the beauty before him. "Nai-bi."

"What does that mean?"

"It means "Pretty woman."

"How do you say pretty man?"

"Tuibitsi."

"Well then...tuibitsi." She whispered into his mouth as he claimed it for another kiss.

Gentle Soul took his time and teased Tempest with his hands and mouth. When his teeth nipped one breast, and then the other one, he felt her bow up in his arms-her breasts straining towards his touch again and again. He settled his head between her legs and dipped his tongue into her moistened center. Tempest gasped her pleasure aloud and he could feel his member throbbing to be inside her, but he held back until he heard her moan and thrash about with her pleasure. When he dipped a finger into her, it didn't take long for her release. She shuddered against him in spasms.

Tempest rode the waves of pleasure until she was almost limp, and that's when Gentle Soul rose above her and entered her slowly. He moved in her in a beautiful constant rhythm. His chest was slick with sweat and his face was flushed with their lovemaking. She could sense him holding back. "Please Gentle Soul, give me all of you…"

Gentle Soul could not hold back any longer with her silent pleas. He moved deeply within her, and each stroke had him closer to spewing his seed in her. "Whiskey, look into my eyes as I take what you offer me."

Tempest gasped at the intimacy, and did as he asked. She rode the waves of pleasure with him.

Chapter Twenty-Seven

Jesus Cruz had searched the surrounding area within a good ten mile radius looking for the Indian who had killed eight of his men. The Indian had looked familiar to him, but he couldn't place what his name was, or how he might have known him. One thing was for sure though, when he found him, he was going to slowly torture him before killing him.

He wondered if the woman was still alive. She was quite a beauty. *What was she doing with an Indian for God's sake? Was she an Injun lover? Or, was she forced to be with the Indian as a captive?* He shook his head to clear his thoughts. One thing was for sure-the Indian highly valued the white woman. Cruz would have to keep that bit of information in mind if they ever met up again...

Heaven

Destiny stood before the Throne of Gods and listened as the God of Love spoke.

"Tempest no longer wants revenge. She is truly happier than she's ever been before in her life." He said proudly.

"Yes, she is, does this mean you'll let her and Gentle Soul stay together?"

"Tempest has to get a divorce before we think about her remaining with Gentle Soul."

Destiny nodded her head in agreement. "May I transport her back to the future she was killed in then?"

The Gods all looked to each other before consenting to her request. The God of Life answered her. "Yes, go ahead and transport her so she can go on with her life, but tell her she's not to kill him."

Destiny whispered in Tempest ear as she slept soundly beside Gentle Soul. Tempest stirred in her sleep, but didn't awaken. Destiny tried talking to her. "Tempest, wake up. It's Destiny; I need to talk to you..."

Tempest groggily opened her heavy eyelids. Destiny hovered above her and was speaking, but Tempest had no idea what she was saying. Tempest rubbed her eyes and sat up straight. "Is it you Destiny? What is it?" she asked.

Destiny floated all around Tempest in a flurry. "Yes Tempest-it's me, come awake now. I have good news."

This grabbed Tempest's attention. "What is it Destiny?" she pulled the furs up to her chin to hide her nakedness.

"I've spoken to the Gods. They have agreed to let me transport you back to the future to get your divorce so you can marry Gentle Soul, but we must hurry."

"But what about Gentle Soul, and Little Doe? I can't just leave him here alone."

"You can take Gentle Soul if you hurry, but Little Doe can remain with your friend for now."

Tempest woke Gentle Soul. "Come my love, Destiny is here to transport us to the future so I can get my divorce, but we must hurry."

Gentle Soul was alert. "I am happy for your divorce Whiskey. I am ready to go with you."

"Gentle Soul as much as I love your body, you can't go naked. Cover yourself and we'll go."

Gentle Soul rose up and put on his deerskin leggings, not bothering to cover his chest. Tempest pulled her Indian dress over head and finger-combed through her long head of hair.

"Are we all ready now?" Destiny asked them.

"Yes. We're ready to go now Destiny." Tempest said.

"Hold hands with each other and me then…"

Once they were all holding hands, Destiny bowed her head and spoke a few words in a foreign language that neither Tempest nor Gentle Soul could make out. "Close your eyes you two." Destiny told them.

Once both of them had closed their eyes, they felt a spinning and pulling sensation catching them up like a tornado. They clung to one another until the world stopped spinning, and they could open their eyes again. Their feet were on hardwood floors now-to be exact, on the floors of her bedroom in her house. Tempest and Gentle Soul opened their eyes to their surroundings. Nothing had changed, Tempest thought.

Gentle Soul walked over to the king-sized bed and sat atop it. "This is nice, is it not?"

Tempest smiled at his excitement. "Yes, it is nice-it's a bed-like under your furs. Doesn't it feel good? Tempest searched the room. "Where is my murdering husband Destiny?"

Chapter Twenty-Six

Brandi fingered the earrings Steve bought her. She worried he might have spent way too much on them. He insisted she take them and put them on, so she did. She knew Steve was going all out on her tonight as they ordered drinks and waited on their food to arrive. He had brought her to the most expensive restaurant in town-Cedar Inn. They had been dating for a couple of months now, but Brando still refused to sleep with him, choosing instead to wait until she was married. She couldn't help but wonder if all this was about getting her to sleep with him. Maybe she was being too critical. After all, Steve had stopped pressuring her like before, and she greatly enjoyed his company, but she wasn't in love with him. He however, professed his love for her every day.

Steve watched Brandi's face. It was always expressive when she thought about things that were important to her, and he wondered now what it was that was so important it had her chewing her bottom lip. *Was she debating whether or not she would let him make love to her?* He could only hope so. He was growing weary of waiting on her, but he did love a challenge. He planned on bedding her tonight, and he wasn't above forcing her either.

"Penny for your thoughts..."

Brandi just smiled sweetly at him and sipped her red wine, holding her glass as close as a lover.

"I was wondering why the special restaurant tonight?"

Steve reached across the table to set her drink down while taking a hand in his. "Tonight is a special night, love. In fact, every night with you is a special night." He said, as he took a box from inside his suit-pocket and held it up to her. "I'm too old to get down on one knee, but Brandi-I love you. I want to wake up with you and go to bed holding you-every night. Will you be my wife pretty girl?"

Brandi was shocked, and words failed her for a moment. She didn't know what she was expecting, but surely not this... "I...don't know what to say Steve. I mean, we've only been dating a few months..."

"Say yes!"

"Oh Steve, I wished it were that that easy. I'm so sorry, but my answer is going to have to be no for now." She could tell her answer disturbed him, but he remained silent afterwards.

"Why?"

"I just think it's too soon for us to be getting married Steve, and besides, Tempest was your whole world...are you really ready for a forever with another woman right now?"

"I am so sick of you questioning me over Tempest! When are you going to realize that she's dead? She's been dead for over two years now Brandi! I let her go the night she died, why can't you let her go after two long years? *Why?!!*"

Brandi shrank away from him. "I can't do this...I don't know what's wrong with you-why you're so angry anytime I mention her name, but I can't do this anymore Steve." Steve watched her step away from him and raise a hand, as if to ward him off.

Steve's face grew a mottled red before her. "Don't do this Brandi-you'll regret it." Brandi left.

Chapter Twenty-Seven

"Destiny, answer me. Where is Steve?"

"Steve is out with Brandi right now, but he'll be here shortly."

"Brandi? As in my friend, Brandi?"

"Yes. He wanted to date her sooner, but she refused until two years had passed, because of her loyalty and friendship to you."

"Oh…" Tempest felt guilty over her assuming the worst. "So they weren't cheating on me then?"

"Only Steve-Brandi has a heart of gold."

Gentle Soul slid off the bed and walked around the bedroom while they talked. He began opening drawers until he found the one with Tempest' bras and panties. He lifted a red lacey thong and inspected it, then held it up."What is this Whiskey?"

Tempest could feel her face flush red. "It's my panties Gentle Soul. Put them back."

A grin appeared on his handsome face. "We take with us. I want to see them on you."

Tempest rolled her eyes. "Men never change."

"We must hurry; Steve will be home soon." Destiny urged them as she floated in between them.

"What's the plan? What are we going to do exactly?"

"You come with me Tempest, and you hide in the closet Gentle Soul, and stay quiet until you hear Steve come into the bedroom. If my plan works right, he won't even come in here, but if it doesn't, then I want you to convince him to give Tempest a divorce any way you want to, but you cannot kill him. Understood?" She waited for Gentle Soul's nod before leaving with Tempest to go downstairs...

Steve was livid with anger. Apparently, he had misjudged Brandi. What a colossal fool he'd been to believe she loved him so much she'd come to his bed. *Women!* He got into his car and burnt rubber on his way home. He thought about how much time and money he'd invested in what he thought was a relationship. Anger boiled inside him at her refusal. He was so sure he had done everything right to convince her to fall into his bed, but he was wrong about her. She now reminded him of Tempest. Tempest was dead but her presence still remained in his life. He hit the steering wheel in frustration. "What the hell do I have to do to get rid of you completely Tempest?"

Tempest heard the sound of Steve's key in the door. She tensed as she waited for him to come inside. Just knowing he was this close to her made her nauseous. Steve laid the mail down on the desk in the entryway before slipping his shoe off and heading towards the kitchen to put on a pot of coffee. By the way he was slamming the cabinet doors; she knew something had made him very angry. She sat in silence and waited on him to come into the living room.

Steve made his cup of coffee and headed towards the living room when he felt it again-those eerie chills he got when he thought a ghost was near-the ghost being Tempest. The hairs on his neck stood straight up as a warning, but he went to the living room anyway. He sat in his favorite chair-his usual spot since they'd bought the house, and turned the TV on.

Tempest and Destiny watched him closely. Destiny motioned for Tempest to walk into the living room now, since she had hid behind the stairwell during his arrival. Tempest shook with fury as she walked the ten steps into the living room, to stand right behind the chair he sat in. Tempest blew into the back of Steve's neck. Steve raised a hand to scratch the itch. It was time to show herself to him. She didn't want to wait any longer.

Steve closed his eyes and rubbed a hand down his face. When he opened his eyes, Tempest stood directly in front of him with a nasty smile on her face. Steve jumped, and kept rubbing his eyes. "Go away Tempest! This is only my imagination!"

"Hello Steve, long time no kill me..." she threw her head back and laughed cynically.

"You're not real. My wife is dead. You're not real..." he kept chanting to convince himself.

Tempest smiled. "Oh but yes, Steve, I'm *very* real! Touch my hand stupid, and you'll see how real I am." Steve shook his head and held one hand with the other one, in his lap. "Touch it, I said!" She bellowed at him.

Steve jumped and did as she asked. As soon as he touched her hand, he jumped back as if electrocuted. "This can't be! You're *alive??* But...I saw your body. I saw them bury you for God's sake! Your face...what happened to your face??"

Tempest leaned down and touched her nose to his. "Oh, you mean when you shot me to death, and my head was half blown off dear?"

"Oh my God...help me Jesus!!" He screamed.

Tempest laughed. "You're asking for God's help after you murdered your own wife?"

Steve covered his ears up."I don't hear you. This isn't real..." he rocked back and forth.

Destiny floated up beside Steve's right ear and whispered. "Oh it's real you murdering bastard! Now listen to what Tempest has to say to you, or I'll wipe the floor with your miserable face!"

"Who's there? What did you do Tempest?" he glared at her accusingly.

"Oh that's just my angel, Destiny. I think I may've rubbed off on her. She never cussed when I met her...ah well, nobody's perfect, right Steve?"

"What do you want from me?" he cried.

"I want a divorce."

"But...you're dead. Why do you need a divorce?"

"That's none of your business. I want you to file for a divorce today Steve."

"But I can't do that. You're dead! Nobody will do a divorce with you dead. I'll look like the biggest fool ever!"

"You are the biggest fool ever!"

"I won't do it, and you can't make me. Leave Tempest-now!"

"I tried to warn you asshole..." Destiny threw him out of his chair and within seconds his face was wiping the living room floor, much to his angry continence.

"You bitch! You're gonna have to kill me, 'cause I aint signing shit- you two hear me? Not one damn thing!"

"Destiny," Tempest spoke up. "Let him go."

Destiny was just now having fun. "Are you sure? I could do this all day ya' know..."

"Just drag him face first up the stairs to the bedroom, then let him go."

Destiny's face fell. "Okay..."

"Oh and Destiny...keep the door locked and remove the phone from the bedroom please..." She smiled at Steve as she went to the room that served as his office.

Tempest could hear his cries as he was dragged up the stairs. They started to fade as she locked herself in his office. She searched through his desk and then went to his computer to pull up divorce papers. After she printed them off she went to the safe behind one of the pictures on the wall and punched in the numbers 'til it opened for her. She would grab what money was left there after she got a pillowcase from their bedroom...

Once Steve arrived in their bedroom, he was relieved when Destiny loosed her hold on him. He got to his knees and then pushed himself up to stand and go sit on their bed. He knew he must be losing his mind. *How could any of this be real*? He thought to himself. Although he couldn't see Destiny, he knew she was still with him in the room. "Are you done now?" he spoke into thin air.

"Oh yes. I'm done with you..." she giggled out.

Steve needed sleep. Yes-that was it-sleep. He was exhausted. He walked to the closet to grab a light blanket and fell back as if burnt when he opened the doors.

Gentle Soul took a step closer to the white man, and his piercing eyes spoke volumes in them. This man deserved to die after what he had done to Tempest. He turned to Destiny first. "Is the *white eyes* going to give her the divorce?" he asked her.

"He refuses to sign anything or get an attorney Gentle Soul. I'm afraid we couldn't make him..." her voice trailed off in pity.

"Does this *white eyes* have a sharp knife here?" he asked Destiny, while Steve's eyes bulged out in fear.

"Yes. In the kitchen."

"Then go Destiny-bring it to me when you have it."

Destiny went to retrieve the knife he requested. Gentle Soul never took his eyes off Steve. "Do you know who I am *white eyes*?"

"You're an Indian." Steve whispered in shock.

"I am not just an Indian. I am the chief of my people, and I am a great warrior. I have claimed Tempest as my own before the central fire, but she cannot be my woman until she gets this divorce from you. I will ask nicely the first time. "Will you give my woman her divorce today?"

"None of this is real- angels, a dead wife, and now an Indian?" Steve laughed bitterly. "I am not signing anything for that crazy bitch! Nothing, you hear me Indian?" He said this while pointing in Gentle Soul's face.

Destiny floated through the locked door, much to the amazement of Steve. She returned with the knife and handed it to Gentle Soul.

Gentle Soul gave his war cry at this, and Steve tried to run away from him, scared out of his mind now. That cry was very real, Steve thought worriedly. He made it to the door, and turned the knob, but it remained locked. Gentle Soul could smell the *white eyes'* fear, and he pounced on it.

Steve could feel the very breath from Gentle Soul as he spoke from directly behind him. "You speak like a foolish man Steve. I asked you nicely the first time, but I won't be so nice again. "I know what you did to Tempest. She told me. What I don't know is why. Tell me now, before I cut out your tongue, why did you kill your own wife?"

Steve didn't believe he was sincere until Gentle Soul pierced his skin with the knife tip. "Wait! Please don't kill me. I'll talk!" It was enough to make him realize it was all really happening, and this man wouldn't hesitate to kill him if he didn't answer him.

Tempest easily opened the door and joined them with papers in her hand. "All he has to do is sign these papers, and the divorce will be granted without any problems." She was alarmed to find Gentle Soul wielding a knife to Steve's throat. "Gentle Soul, what are you doing? You can't kill him!"

"Answer me, why did you kill Tempest?"

"Because she wanted a divorce and I didn't want to be left broke." He admitted like the slime he was.

Gentle Soul grimaced in disgust at him, but still held the knife to his throat. "Sign the papers if you want to live another day."

Tempest watched him sign and after she signed, she grabbed a pillow case to take downstairs. "Thanks Steve. By the way, I hope you understand...I'm taking all the gold in the safe with me. Goodbye..."

"NOoooooo!! Please Tempest-I need that for money!" Steve reached to get a hold of her, but Gentle Soul stayed his hand upon her, by catching both of Steve's hands in one of his hands, gripping it tightly. "Try to touch my woman again, and I will scalp you right here, then cut out your cowardly heart to feed to the fowls of the sky."

Whiskey Woman

Steve whimpered in fear, and Tempest winked at him in pure satisfaction. It had been one of the best days she had ever had, and Tempest would always carry the look of fear on Steve's face with her through life and smile upon the memory.

Chapter Twenty-Eight

Gentle Soul and Tempest sat together at the table Gentle Soul had made for Tempest since arriving at his village. He thought Tempest would use it to write, but so far, all she had done was prepare their dinner and eat upon it.

Ever since Destiny had dropped the two of them off at his village on her way back to heaven, Gentle Soul became worried about Tempest. She was too quiet for a woman who had just visited the husband who murdered her so callously.

"How are you feeling Whiskey?" Gentle Soul put his arm around her.

"Fine." She uttered with a shaky breath.

"You say fine, but your body says something else. You shake. Is it in fear? He will never hurt you again. This promise I vow to you…"

"Fear?" she asked. "No, I don't fear him. He's a heartless coward! My body shakes in loathsome anger Gentle Soul." She arose and paced the floors.

Gentle Soul wished to calm his woman, but he knew it might help for her to let her feelings out here with him where she was safe, so he sat quietly and merely listened.

"I cannot sit back and watch him hurt Brandi. My God-she's just a foolish young woman! She's not match for him Gentle Soul. What if he gets angry again? He got by with killing me. Who's to say he wouldn't get by with it a second time?"

Gentle Soul's heart fell a little to see her so worried. "I should've killed him when I had the chance. I'm sorry I didn't."

"Destiny said The Gods wouldn't allow it Gentle Soul. Don't blame yourself. You can't go against The Gods."

"Why do The Gods protect him? He's a waste of flesh, heart and spirit. He deserves death."

"I agree Gentle Soul." Tempest reached out to hold his hand. "Lets us not be sad today. After all, I am a free woman now-free to marry a chief." She spoke impishly.

Gentle Soul smiled wickedly. "I am a chief. It is good that you found me when you did."

"Oh really? Please tell me more…"

Gentle Soul mimicked a serious expression on his face. "As a chief, I was in high demand for single maidens…"

Tempest punched his arm playfully. "Ahh, I didn't realize you were that popular among your people. I'm sure you grew weary of the women throwing themselves at you…"

"Yes. It was hard to deal with so many admirers every day."

"Well then, I'm thinking you should be grateful to me for saving you from all those women.

Gentle Soul laughed with her. "Thank you Whiskey, for saving me."

Tempest got up and positioned herself between Gentle Souls legs. She bent her head and kissed him deeply. "I love you chief."

Gentle Soul thrilled to her kiss. Her hair fell all around him like a glorious curtain. "My woman, your beauty surpasses the colors of a sun rising." He kissed her back eagerly. "I want to marry you soon Whiskey Woman."

"We have so much to do Gentle Soul. It will take me awhile to do what's needed before we get married."

"What is more important than getting married, love?"

"Nothing is as important as our marriage, but there are things I need to get done, and things we surely need before we get married."

"Tell me these things woman."

"We need another room built so Little Doe can sleep in her own room. Also, we need more things for the lodge to make it feel like home, and I want to decorate your lodge to reflect our marriage together. I know it's silly, but…"

"Your wants are never silly Whiskey. I have an idea."

Tempest perked up. "You do? What is it? Tell me Gentle Soul."

"I will take you to a town where you can buy all things you want. Is that good enough?"

"Oh Gentle Soul…" she kissed him feverishly while he laughed. "I would love that! Yes! Thank you so much!!!"

Gentle Soul had never seen his woman so happy. "Whiskey Woman, there is one problem I must speak to you before we go."

Tempest stilled. "What is it Gentle Soul?" she gnawed her bottom lip.

Gentle Soul bowed his head in shame. "I have no money Tempest. My people trade with horses, but this general store only takes cash. I am shamed to admit that to my woman. All your needs should be taken care of by me."

Tempest felt her heart dip within her chest. She placed both hands on either side of his face as she forced his face up to look into his eyes. "Gentle Soul. You have already provided me with all my needs, and a child to call mine too. You have nothing to be ashamed about-*nothing!* I took all the money left from the safe. That money is *ours* Gentle Soul, and we can use that for all the things we just want, okay? I love you. Why get rid of your many horses, when I have nowhere else to spend this money?"

Gentle Soul knew he'd have to weigh her words against his sense of pride before agreeing with this. "I will go think on this and when I come back, I will bring Little Doe home."

Whiskey Woman

Tempest brushed her lips against his temple. "Go do what you must my chief. I will clean the lodge and prepare us a dinner."

"I love you Whiskey Woman-never forget that."

Gentle Soul took Black Wing out to the gravesite of his family and his late wife. He let Black Wing graze while he both thought, and talked about the decision he had to make. "Father, it is I, Gentle Soul. I have questions and I need your help."

Gentle Soul felt a gust of wind, and he wondered if it was a sign that his father could hear him. "Mother, I need your help too. I can't ask Silent Speaks, as I have moved on with another woman, but I mean her no disrespect. It is our custom not the mention the deads' name, so I won't say it again and pray the wind carries it away."

The last time I came here, I asked for a strong, brave, and beautiful woman to come to me, and the Gods did bring her to me. I am thankful for such a woman as she has turned out to be. She cares for my people, and she loves deeply. But, I cannot provide for her the many things she wants. I can provide her needs, but I fear it is not enough for her. She should have so much more than what I can provide her with. I ask that you give me a sign of whether I should marry her now, and use her money to let her buy what she wants, or wait until I can pay for them myself, on my own. We are a very proud people, so it goes against my belief to let my woman buy what she wants, as I want to buy what she wants by myself. Please give me a sign of what to do..."

Gentle Soul kneeled between the graves of his father and mother and closed his eyes, as if in prayer, and began to sing as he waited for a response to his question.

The wind picked up and he had to shield his face from the dirt that blew all around him. With his hand covering his eyes, he heard a voice speak to him. The wind ceased immediately.

"My son, it is I, and your mother. Look up at us son." He spoke in a soft commanding voice.

Gentle Soul trembled at his father's voice so close to him. He put his hand down and opened his eyes to see the two of them floating in the air above him, on a cloud. He wiped his eyes, but they were still there. "Father, Mother! It is good to hear from you and see you both!" he cried.

"We were able to come because of Destiny intervening for you to the Gods. Son, listen to my words: Money is nothing. It is meant to spend. Do not despise small beginnings. You are rich in everything that counts, and money is only temporal, so let your woman use it to help you both. Pride goes before a fall son. Don't let this stand in the way of your happiness."

"Yes Father, I hear you. Thank you for answering me. My heart was heavy today, but it feels right again. I love you Father, and Mother."

Gentle Souls Mother spoke up, "Son, though trouble may come, know that we and heaven, are with you all the time. Go now, and love your woman that The Gods have sent for you. She is a good *pia* to Little Doe, and she will give you great strong sons as well. I love you my son, but we must leave now."

"I love you both. Thank you for answering my cries. Thank Destiny for me too."

Gentle Soul said a prayer and rose up to his feet. All would be well. It was good that he had come here to seek answers, but now was the time to go back and tell Tempest of all that had happened. There was no reason they had to wait to get married now, so he hurried back to their village.

Gentle Souls heart swelled with excitement. "Nothing will stop us now Whiskey Woman."

Chapter Twenty-Nine

The whole village was busy with talk of Tempest and Gentle Souls wedding to take place during the spring. Although they both wanted to get married sooner, Tempest preferred a wedding when it was warmer. Gentle Soul was proud of his people, the way in which they accepted her and Tempest was happily busy working beside the women to make everything perfect for their big day just two months away. Gentle Soul had promised her that they would go to town before the wedding, and she was glad he seemed to accept her money without arguing. They lay together the night before their trip into town and held each other close as they talked about their dreams. Gentle Soul wanted to build them a new home that was more like what Tempest was accustomed to, and Tempest wanted to help other women in the village who couldn't afford some of life's finer things to help make their daily jobs less arduous.

Because this wasn't the first time they had talked about what they would like to get from town, Gentle Soul had made them a fine cart to hold everything they might get on their trip. He already had the team of horses ready for the trip in the morning, and among them, was a very pregnant Black Wing. She would be a new mama in just two more weeks, and Gentle Soul planned on giving her baby to Tempest when it was born, as a bride-gift to her. Life was good, and Gentle Soul didn't think he could be happier than he was right now.

Tempest noticed his smile. "Is my man happy now?"

"Your man is very happy Whiskey Woman, and you? Are you happy?" he beseeched her.

"I'd be happier if you'd ravish me and take full advantage of me, Chief."

Whiskey Woman

Gentle Soul didn't miss the glint in her big brown eyes. "My woman has a big appetite for me, heh?" He cajoled her as he began nipping her neck and shoulder.

"I only have a big appetite for you, Chief." She quit talking then, as she lost herself in his delicate kisses along her collar bone.

Gentle Soul loved the taste of her skin. She tasted like sweet berries. He stopped to remove her clothing and then his own, before taking the long braid out of her hair. Her hair looked like fire as the flames threw a light into it from the fire he had built. It lay spread out all around him and he bent his head to smell it too.

Tempest laughed. "What are you doing Gentle Soul?"

"I'm putting you in my senses Whiskey, so that when we grow old, I will have this memory of you-of us, together, right now..."

Tempest felt a tear come to her eyes. "How can you be so formidable in wars, yet so very thoughtful with me?"

"I never choose to war, but I do choose to be with you Whiskey. You're better than the breath I breathe."

Tempest felt her heart do a flip-flop then. She wanted this man like none other, and now.

"Love me Gentle Soul." She pleaded. "Love me now, and don't let go of me until morning."

Gentle Soul and Tempest ate breakfast with Little Doe before they left that morning for town. Little Doe wanted to go with them, but it would be a trip that would be too long for her to travel right now. Besides, Tempest didn't want to take a chance of Little Doe getting sick in the cold weather.

They arrived in town four hours later and Gentle Soul was overjoyed to see Tempest so happy to be there. After securing their makeshift wagon, they entered the general store together. Two women were up front checking customers out when they arrived. Both women stopped talking long enough to stare at Tempest and Gentle Soul. Tempest noticed both their faces had turned white in fear at having an Indian in their store, and it angered her greatly.

Tempest spoke to both of them. "Excuse me, can one of you two ladies help me?" she asked politely.

While one couldn't seem to find her voice, the other one made up for. "We don't serve *Injuns* here." She sneered nastily.

Not wanting to embarrass Tempest, Gentle Soul turned to leave the store, but Tempest stopped him by grabbing his arm. "No. You will stay with me." She told him.

Tempest turned to the offending woman once more. "I'm sorry you feel that way Miss, because I have to spend fifty thousand dollars somewhere..."

The woman gasped at such an unheard of amount of money. Her attitude changed immediately.

"But... but how did you get so much money? That's unheard of!" she sputtered.

Tempest casually answered her. "My husband here gets a lot of money for scalping people; don't you dear?" she smiled sweetly at Gentle Soul, while the rude woman gasped in fear.

Gentle Soul wanted to laugh, but he knew he must keep a straight face for Tempest' sake. "Yes white woman. He noticed the wheat-blonde color of the owner's hair and then added, "We get extra pay for blonde hair-like this woman's."

"Oh please sir, don't take mine. Shop here as long as you want. I promise not to bother you, and I'll help you both all I can, but please don't scalp me." She trembled as she waited for a response.

"I will stay my husband's hand upon your head as long as you help us get what we came for."

The woman let out a pent up breath of relief. "Thank you."

Tempest spent two hours buying everything she wanted, while Gentle Soul stacked it in the wagon. Both Tempest, and the two other women had to help load the bathtub onto the wagon. Tempest was overjoyed with everything they had bought, but she was getting unusually tired. She feared she may have caught a virus. After all, she had been getting sick to her stomach for the past week every morning. She had just paid the store keeper and was headed out to climb onto the wagon when a dizzy spell hit her hard. Her legs gave out and everything turned black.

Tempest woke up minutes later, in Gentle Souls lap. "You fainted." he said.

Tempest' eyes grew as big as saucers in her face. "I did? Why?" she looked to him for answers.

Gentle Soul couldn't take any chances with Tempest getting ill. "I don't know little one, but we shall see the town's doctor and find out." He told her as he helped her down to the ground, then led her to the doctor's office.

Gentle Soul went to stay with the wagon while the doctor looked her over. He had wanted to be with her, but she insisted on him staying with the wagon in fear of people robbing them of the goods they had just bought, so he did.

An hour later, the doctor helped Tempest back to the wagon. He didn't seem to care that there was an Indian waiting on her as he approached Gentle Soul and shook his hand.

"Hello there, I'm the town's doctor, Mr. Thomas Caldwell, but you may call me Tommy."

Gentle Soul took his hand in his for a shake. "And my name is Gentle Soul. It is nice to meet you Tommy. How is Tempest? He asked the doctor, concerned.

The doctor smiled broadly. "Well, I reckon that depends on you, young man..."

"Me?"

"Yes. Tempest here is pregnant. I'd judge her to be around two months now, and she's doing great. Make sure she gets plenty of rest though, and no lifting heavy objects. Is that a problem?" he asked them both.

Tempest watched for Gentle Soul's reaction at the news, but he didn't show any-his eyes were hooded like long before, when they first met.

"It won't be a problem Doctor. She will be treated very well, I vow it to you."

Gentle Soul helped her up onto the wagon's seat, and thanked the doctor.

"If you need anything Tempest, don't hesitate to come back."

Tempest only nodded at him. "Th-thank you doctor; I will."

Neither one of them spoke a word on the way back to their village.

Gentle Soul thought about the baby he had lost. His heart ached. He couldn't stand to lose another one, so he knew he must not get too excited about this one.

Tempest felt the tears slide down both cheeks, but she refused to rub them off. *Damn him!*

Chapter Thirty

The winter had proved to be a mild one, and Tempest was glad. Gentle Soul stayed busy for the next three months, building their new lodge, which looked more like a new house every day. Tempest was showing now, and her baby had started to kick faintly in her belly. It was something she should have been sharing with her husband to be, but he didn't want any part of their baby it seemed. Tempest was hurt to her very core. She couldn't understand why Gentle Soul had put such distance between them since finding out she was pregnant with his child. It seemed like they had it all-they had Little Doe, the respect of their people, a beautiful home that reflected what she was used to, fine eating utensils, a bath tub, an outhouse, and even a push-peddle sewing machine. Tempest didn't lack for anything except Gentle Soul's attention and closeness. She had witnessed in the past, the way Gentle Soul would play with Little Doe, but even that had stopped. Tempest had stayed, to try and get past all of it, but spring was just coming in, and Gentle Soul continued to make excuses to her as to why he was never home. She knew now, it wouldn't help if she did stay longer, in fact, it would only hurt her worse. So, she made up her mind finally, to leave as soon as she had the chance. The only problem was, she couldn't take Little Doe with her. It would be dangerous enough for her to be traveling alone, without adding her daughter to it. She couldn't bear the thought of anything happening to Little Doe. All she had to do now was wait for the right opportunity to leave.

Two more months past before her opportunity came up. It was already May and Tempest was now seven months pregnant. Black Wing's baby was now four months old. Gentle Soul never had the time to take her to see the baby, and that hurt too. She made it to Loving Hearts lodge one day to ask her to keep Little Doe for her for a few hours. She claimed she just needed rest, so Loving Heart wouldn't worry over her. Gentle Soul was out hunting, so she knew she would have a few hours to get to where she was going without him stopping her, but truth be told, he probably wouldn't really stop her. No, he would be glad, she was sure of it.

Tempest held back her tears and fears when she left Little Doe, knowing it would be the last time she saw her lovely daughter. Instead, she busied herself with packing only the essentials: tooth brush, soap and rose water, clothes, and food enough for a few days journey. Then she snuck out and prepared Black Wing for traveling. She tied her belongings onto the horse and said a silent goodbye to everyone she had come to love, as well as Gentle Soul. Once she sat atop Black Wing, she let the horse have his way to go where he wanted, and interestingly enough, Black Wing rode in the direction of town...

Meanwhile, Gentle Soul was dressing out the deer that he had killed. Dancing Eyes helped him clean the meat and cut it, so Tempest would be spared that chore. Dancing Eyes had never been one to pry into other's business, but for his chief's sake, he knew it was high time to say something to him. "Gentle Soul, we have known each other many years, yes?"

"Yes, Dancing Eyes."

"Haven't we loved one another as good as brother's, my friend?"

"Yes. We are same as brother's, Dancing Eyes. Why do you ask these silly questions?"

"I see more than you tell me. Your woman's fire in her eyes has left her because of you."

Gentle Soul growled. "You see nothing brother, but what you imagine."

Dancing Eyes shook his head. "You should be heap happy with news of your first child."

"It's not my first child. The first child is dead, and is walking above the clouds with it's mother Silent Speaks."

Dancing Eyes bowed his head in sorrow. "I am sorry you lost them both, but Gentle Soul, you must go on with your life now. Your woman needs you now, more than ever."

"You don't think I know that?" he asked incredibly angry. "Why do you think I have distanced myself from her while she carries our baby? I do it to keep her safe, and the baby too. I can't lose another wife and child, Dancing Eyes. I can't!"

"You're a fool Gentle Soul. Tempest is stronger than you give her credit for. Don't let your fear override your love for her, because you might just lose her by ignoring her so."

"What is that supposed to mean?" he asked bitingly.

"It means stop being so blind and foolish. Go to your woman now, and tell her all you have told me. If you truly love her, then you must step up and be the man she fell in love with. Right now you're just a coward." And with that said, Dancing Eyes turned to walk away from him.

"I do love her. Heaven help me, I do, but I'm scared..."

Dancing Eyes turned around a few feet ahead of him. "Then go talk to your woman now, before she has the good sense to leave you brother."

Gentle Soul watched his friend walk away from him and be swallowed up by the trees and thicket that surrounded them both. He thought about their conversation. Dancing Eyes was right. He had been foolish to ignore Tempest like he did. After the hunt, he would return to the village tonight and tell her everything that was in his heart, and marry her that night. He prayed it wasn't too late for her to forgive him...

Tempest was only an hour away from town, but she was hurting in her back. She was so tired. She never imagined she could get so tired just traveling. The baby was leaping in her belly now, and she liked watching her belly take on different shapes as the baby grew stronger each day. She had stopped frequently along the trial to rest and nibble on food. The sun was going down now, so she knew she needed to push on until she got to town, but the pain pulsated through her. If she were a man, she'd stop and sleep, but since she wasn't, she pushed onward until she could see the lights in town at a distance. A few times, she had heard noises that seemed as if she was being followed, but each time she looked back, she saw nothing. It must be her imagination, she thought wearily.

Finally, she made it into town, and headed towards the good doc's office. She hated to bother him so late, but he was the only hope she had of getting some help. She dismounted and walked to the door of his office. No answer. She looked up at the two-story building, and it dawned on her that he must live upstairs. So, she walked into the alleyway to climb the stairs, when she felt a hand suddenly wrap around her muffled screams. "Don't say a word, or scream. If you do, I'll cut that bastard baby right out of your belly, ya hear me?" the voice asked.

Tempest nodded a yes. She knew that voice-it was medicine woman's.

"Good. Now turn around slowly, and don't try anything."

Tempest turned around slowly, until her eyes rested on Medicine Womans face. Medicine Woman removed her hand, and Tempest remained silent, in fear for the baby. Medicine woman spoke up. "I've been watching you. I'm glad you decided to leave the village white eyes. I guess Gentle Soul didn't like the thought of being a daddy again, did he?"

Again? What was the crazed woman thinking now, she wondered.

"I see Gentle Soul forgot to mention that part of his story to you." She laughed, like it was funny. "Gentle Soul's wife was raped before they broke her neck and stabbed the baby inside of her mama."

Tempest froze, as she thought about the horror of that happening, but still, she remained silent.

"You can speak now, if you know how to whisper."

"What do you want? Money? I have money, if that's what you want..."

"Oh I'll get your money alright. I'm going to make Gentle Soul bring it to us-don't you worry about that missy!" she laughed.

"To *us?*"

Whiskey Woman

Medicine woman wore a smirk on her face. "Yes, us...I have new friends thanks to you and Gentle Soul."

Tempest watched her as she spoke over her shoulder. "You all can come out now. I've got her, but you'll have to take her to the lodge yourselves."

Two men came out of the darkness. They were undoubtedly comancheros-both of them. Tempest recognized the one of them. It was Jesus Cruz-the same man who tried to take her when she first met Gentle Soul.

His eyes roamed over all of her body. She felt her heart lurch when he spoke. "Senorita, it is good to see you again. Your lover killed seven of my best men, and now I'm going to give him payback."

"Please," Tempest begged, "Just take my money. There's lots of it. Just take it and leave me alone. I'm pregnant. Do you not have any decency sir?" she pleaded.

Jesus just laughed. "Decency? Is that what you call it? No. I have none. I will take your money senorita, but only after I have bedded you, and rid the world of a bastard child."

Tempest was enraged. "Don't you dare lay a hand on me, or else..." she threatened him.

"Or else, what? Your lover is not here to save you this time Senorita. I wouldn't be so nasty if I were you. Besides, you might enjoy having a real man to rut with between your legs..." he sneered at her.

"You will never ride me you piece of filth! I'll die before I let you do that, or hurt my baby." Tempest spat in his face, and was rewarded with a blow to her head.

Jesus swiped at the spit on his face. "I see you like to fight. Good. I will mount you roughly."

Jesus reached into his pocket and dug out a few coins. "Here Medicine Woman-You have done your job quite nicely, now leave the lady and I to be alone." Medicine woman took the coins and with one final nasty look at Tempest, she hurried away.

"Casteel, come forth and show your face to the lady."

Tempest watched as the other man came forward with head bent downward as not to show his face. She felt cold chills as she looked at him, and had the strange feeling she knew this man, but how?

"Just call me Steve, Cruz. Steve is my real name." And just then, Steve looked up and Tempest found herself face-to-face with her ex-husband! Tempest felt the world close in on her and she fainted. Steve was smiling like an opossum. "Give her to me. I will take her back where she came from and make damned sure she doesn't live this time, or her bastard baby."

"How so, white man?"

"I finally figured out how she gets angels to take her places...but I got a rather naughty angel to help me...one that fell from Heaven..." he boasted rather proudly.

"How soon are you going to take her?"

"As soon as the angel comes to us."

Destiny came to Gentle Soul on his way back from hunting. He was surprised to see her come to him without being summoned, and he felt the hairs stand up on the back of his neck when he saw her face. She was pale and gaunt. Something bad was wrong.

"Destiny, what is wrong?"

"It's Tempest-she's gone Gentle Soul."

Gentle Soul stilled his movements. "Gone? What do you mean, gone?"

"She's been planning this for weeks now, but I had hoped you would wake up sooner than you did. You are such an ass, Gentle Soul!"

Gentle Soul blinked. "Where is she?"

"She was on her way back to stay with the doc, but Medicine Woman found her and held her until the comanchero Jesus could get her in his hands..."

"I'll kill him for this!"

"Wait! That's not all. Then Steve showed up and he has her now."

"Her ex-husband, Steve?"

"Yes-that's the one."

"Where did he take her Destiny?"

"Oh Gentle Soul. This is so bad...he had a fallen angel transport him to the alleyway where the doc's office is, and he's just waiting for the same angel to return and take her back for good." She cried.

Gentle Soul was stunned. "You must take me to her Destiny. You must. *Now!*"

Destiny held his hand and they left. It only took moments for them to arrive, but it seemed like an eternity to Gentle Soul. He thought about how he had ignored Tempest and guilt tore at him. He had been selfish, and scared, but not as scared as he was right now. He would give his life to turn things around for them. He just hoped they reached her before the bad angel came to take her away. He said a prayer to the God of Life, and the God of Judgment. He hoped they were listening...

Chapter Thirty-One

Steve surveyed the way Tempest looked pregnant. "So, your injun-lover got you knocked up, did he? She saw the contempt in his wild eyes.

"Why do this Steve? What could you possibly stand to gain from taking me?"

"Are you serious? You made us get that damn divorce. I couldn't touch your money anymore. I tried to tell you to leave it alone, but you just had to come back into my life, didn't you? You messed up everything! Everything! Brandi won't have anything to do with me now, all because of you!" He shook her hard enough to make her cry.

"Save your tears bitch, 'cause you'll not get any pity from me."

As he was speaking, an angel appeared in the midst of them. He was big and ugly, for sure. His whole body smoked from the flames he came from, and Tempest could smell the stench of burning flesh. He floated closer to her, to get a better look at her. "Ahh, you must be Tempest." He said.

Tempest couldn't tear her eyes away from him. She was horrified by him. She flinched when he drew so close his breath fell on her. "Are we ready to go now?" he asked all of them.

Cruz spoke up. "Not so fast. I have been cheated of her certain charms before, but I will gladly hand over the money for one romp with her Steve. What do ya say?" he asked Steve.

"What a splendid idea Cruz. Hand me the money up front, and then you may do whatever you wish except kill her. I alone will have that pleasure."

As Cruz tried to take her from Steve, Tempest fought him like a mad woman out of her head. She screamed, kicked, and bit him repeatedly, but he laughed as he delivered two more blows to her head and face. Finally, with the help of the angel, who held her down, he unzipped his fly and with his knife, he cut her doeskin dress fully apart.

Tempest felt the cold night air on her flesh exposed for all to see. Her shame was great, but her hatred even stronger. "Take your filthy hands off of me you pervert!"

Cruz laughed. "I love a woman who likes to fight, especially when she cannot win." He spoke to her.

Tempest felt one of his hands paw at her breasts, and she cringed. Since the angel held her down, she couldn't fight anymore. "So this is what you're reduced to. Is raping a defenseless, pregnant woman something you pride yourself on?"

Cruz was busy stroking himself harder. "Shut up! Shut up now, or I'll cut that bastard baby right out of you before I have you."

Tempest couldn't bear any of it anymore. She looked pleadingly towards her ex-husband, "Steve please, just do me a favor and kill me now. Don't wait til this monster cuts my baby out of me."

Steve never even hesitated. "Why don't you show her no mercy and take the baby first, then rape her and give her to me. I'm sure she'll welcome death then Cruz."

Cruz knelt down on the ground where she lay with her legs opened up and poised himself above her to take her when a wind came so hard it knocked him over. "What the...?"

Tempest couldn't see anything because she had closed her eyes against what she knew was coming when he got ready to rape her. She opened her eyes to find him beside her and she was confused, until she turned her eyes towards the angel who lost his grip on her. Standing right behind the angel was Destiny. "Go back to hell now, or The Gods will hunt you down and make your stay in hell even worse than what it has been." The angel let go and vanished into thin air.

"Oh my God-Destiny! It's you! You came to help me! Oh thank God! Wait-where's Cruz?"

Whiskey Woman

"Right behind you Bitch!" Cruz had a gun in his hand, trained on the back of her head. "Don't move, or I'll blow your soul to hell."

Steve chose then to try and leave the scene, but before he had taken two steps, Gentle Soul spoke up. "Where do you think you're going?"

Steve turned to face Gentle Soul. "Let me leave here, and I'll never bother Tempest again."

Gentle Soul's eyes darkened dangerously as he noticed his woman's dress was hanging completely open for all to see her nakedness. "Trust me white eyes, neither of you will *ever* bother Tempest again, this I vow."

Steve looked at Cruz. "I will give you half of this money if you kill the injun." Tempest heart stopped. "No!!! You can't kill him! Please. I'll do whatever you want, but please don't kill him."

Cruz heard the offer and hesitated. That was all Tempest needed. She reached into her sock for the knife held there since the day they had visited her ex-husband and sunk it deeply into Cruz. Steve dropped the gun and ran as fast as he could from Gentle Soul, but it did him no good. Gentle soul buried an arrow into the man's heart, as he turned to see how close Gentle Soul was to him. Steve was dead. Gentle Soul went to stand beside Tempest as Cruz began to crawl on his belly like the snake he was. Gentle Soul turned to Tempest and gathered her in his arms.

"You came for me." Why?" she asked.

"I was a fool Whiskey Woman. I was scared of losing the baby. Silent Speaks lost our baby and her life thanks to Cruz and his men. I was afraid for you and scared over the baby. I thought I could better protect you both by staying away-protect myself too. I was wrong. Please forgive me. I love you Whiskey Woman. "

"Oh Gentle Soul, I love you too. I didn't know what was happening to us. I'm so glad you came for me."

"I will always come for you Whiskey."

Whiskey Woman

Gentle Soul watched Cruz try to slither away from them. He walked over to him. "Where is Medicine Woman?"

"You're too late. He said with a hysterical laugh."

"Too late for what?"

"She's back in your village. The other angel sent her back. She's going to take Little Doe with her."

Tempest grew cold. "Oh my God-Noooo!!!" She screamed.

Cruz's mouth slackened open, to display that he had finally died.

Tempest asked Destiny to transport them back to the village immediately. All three of them held hands and within minutes were back on the backside of the house Gentle Soul had built for Tempest and Little Doe. It was hard to see in the blackness of night. Tempest hoped Gentle Soul's eyesight was better than her own.

Gentle Soul whispered to Tempest. "Go inside the house and remain there until I bring Little Doe back to you."

Tempest wouldn't have it. "No way-I'm coming with you Gentle Soul. She's my daughter too!"

Gentle Soul looked to Destiny. "Please hold her here Destiny. I don't want anything to happen to her and the baby while I'm gone. Okay?" he asked her.

Tempest had no choice in the matter when Destiny forced her into the house with her.

"Gentle Soul, if you don't come back, I'm going to kill you!"

Chapter Thirty-Two

Medicine Woman had just tied Woman of Sorrow up. Dancing eyes hadn't made it back from the hunt yet, but she knew she had better hurry. If she was lucky, both Tempest and Gentle Soul were dead right now, so all she had to worry about was getting some of Little Does things packed to take her with her. Cruz would gladly take Little Doe off her hands and pay handsomely for the little girl. Medicine Woman could use that money to start a new life for herself. She could care less what the comanchero chose to do with the little girl. Her conscience wasn't easily bothered anymore. She had become a very bitter woman.

Little Doe sniffled and sobbed, like a crybaby. "Stop that Little Doe! Stop or I will put leather to your backside!"

Little Doe tried hard to stop, but she had no control over her fears of the Medicine Woman, and she knew she was evil. "I want my Mama..." she cried pitifully.

Medicine woman grabbed her by her hair and shook her. "Tempest is not your mama-and she's never coming back for you!"

This only brought fresh tears to the frightened child.

Gentle Soul heard Little Doe's cries before he knew where she was-inside Dancing Eye's lodge. He peered inside the house through a flap in the back of the lodge, where he saw that Woman of Sorrow had been tied up and gagged. His anger ran hot as he watched Medicine Woman pull Little Does hair. She was hurting her, and she knew it.

"Let Little Doe go Medicine Woman, and you won't be hurt." He said through the flap.

Whiskey Woman

Medicine Woman jerked Little Doe closer to her when she heard Gentle Soul speak. "Stay back Gentle Soul, or I'll cut her pretty little throat." She held a knife to Little Doe's neck as she spoke.

"What do you want Medicine Woman?"

"You have nothing to offer me Gentle Soul. You shouldn't have sent me away."

"Let the child go, and we'll talk about you coming back."

"Ohh, so now you want to be nice to me-now that I have what your white-eyes woman wants to claim as her own!"

Gentle Soul knew he was dealing with a crazed woman now. There would be no reasoning with her, so he had only one option: grab Little Doe as fast as he could. He walked around the lodge to stand in front of the flap to the entryway.

"Come on in Gentle Soul. We have a nice surprise for you chief." She almost purred to him.

Gentle Soul came through the flap and found himself face to face with Medicine Woman. Medicine Woman wasn't prepared for him lunging at her so fast. He quickly grabbed Little Doe and turn to run with her, when he felt the knife sink into his back-repeatedly. He went down quickly, and his whole world went black.

Tempest heard the screams of Little Doe and without permission from Destiny, she ran out of the lodge towards her screams. Little Doe ran into her arms and cried pitifully. "Father is hurt, Mama."

Tempest handed Little Doe to Destiny and ran as fast as her legs would carry her. She ran into the lodge and found Willow standing there with a gun. She had shot and killed Medicine Woman. Woman of Sorrow still sat as she was-tied up, but when Tempest looked at her, Willow was freeing her.

"Tempest, Gentle Soul is dying. I tried to stop it, but Medicine Woman was too fast. I am so sorry. You have been a good mother. I will leave you alone now." Although she was sincere, all Tempest could concentrate on was Gentle Soul, lying in a pool of his own blood, gasping for air.

Tempest fell on the ground beside him and lifted his head to rest in her lap. "You cannot die Gentle Soul. I forbid it-you hear me? Damn it-I love you! We have things to do. You promised you'd marry me!"

"Kamakutu-nu." He whispered.

"I love you too Gentle Soul." Tempest prayed like she'd never prayed before, but she knew the moment he left her-she could feel his absence from her. "NOoooooo!!!" she wailed, as she rocked back and forth. "Oh God No!!!" she bellowed, as she leaned down to kiss his forehead.

Destiny could hear Tempest's screams all the way to the lodge, and her heart wrenched for her. She wanted to go for her, but she didn't want Little Doe to see what had happened, so she remained in the lodge.

Tempest had no idea how long she wailed for Gentle Soul. Time had no meaning now. She sobbed until she could cry no longer. The people had heard her cries and one by one came to gather outside the lodge. After hearing what had happened, they mourned with Tempest. Woman of Sorrow tried to pull her away from Gentle Soul, but Tempest only clung harder. She tried to reason with her.

"Come Whiskey Woman. Gentle Soul would not want you to grieve so. You are carrying his baby."

Just then, Dancing Eyes pushed through the crowd to kneel beside Gentle Soul and Tempest. "Gentle Soul was very brave. He died an honorable death. I will stay with you tonight, but you must let the people carry him to prepare his body for burial..." he urged her gently.

Tempest raised her tear-streaked face to Dancing Eyes. "Would you let Woman of Sorrow go so easily, my brother?"

Dancing Eyes lowered his gaze and gave no answer, which was answer enough for Tempest.

"Make a pallet of many furs outside our lodge, and I will let the people carry him there, so all can see him. We will talk more then."

"Aye-we will do as you wish Whiskey Woman, but please allow Woman of Sorrow to help you back to your lodge."

Woman of Sorrow helped Tempest up, and walked with her to the lodge she and Gentle Soul shared. Tempest asked her to take Little Doe back to her lodge until she could come back for her.

Tempest waited for everyone to gather before she spoke again. All eyes were on her as she stood there, by herself. "My people, it is with a heavy heart that I speak to you this night, but I know I must speak. As you know, Gentle Soul and I planned on getting married in a short time, but he was slain by one of our own-Medicine Woman. I'm sure you all have your own way of dealing with the dead, but we aren't going to do things that way tonight. No, we are going to watch the God's give Gentle Soul back to me, and back to you this night…"

Tempest could hear the crowd gasp at her strange words. "Please don't pity me, because I have not lost Gentle Soul as some of you think. I call on the God of Love, the God of Life, and the God of Judgment, to come to me now, and I ask for everyone here to hold hands and pray with me."

Destiny came to float beside her, and the people shrieked in disbelief at seeing an angel appear to them. Some marveled at Tempest's ability to call forth angels and Gods. Tempest raised her voice, and the people did too.

They were all praying when the wind picked up and swirled around them all. Tempest raised her voice above the sound. "I ask the Gos to restore Gentle Soul, and give him life again, to become my husband, and be a father to our children. Come God's, and do this thing for me, and I shall not ask anything else of you. Breathe life back into Gentle Soul, and restore him to be exactly as he was before he was stabbed." The crowd couldn't believe their eyes. Above them, were three Gods, gathered together, and it was the God of Life that spoke. "We have heard your prayer towards us, and because you have risked your life and stood firmly in your belief, we shall grant his life back, as well as let you remain together forever. Be blessed little one."

Gentle Soul's wound closed up and everyone cheered. He opened his eyes as if he had merely been asleep and smiled at Tempest. Tempest leaned down and kissed him, as her tears fell on his face. "How are you feeling, my love?" she asked.

Gentle Soul slowly stood up and gathered her into his arms as he spoke loud enough for his people to hear him. "My friends, today has been a day like no other. I didn't think I would be coming back, but because of my woman, the Gods have allowed it. Thank you all for your prayers."

The people sent up many thanks. Destiny was happy for them both, and quietly made her exit back into Heaven.

Tempest spoke up. "Gentle Soul, I think it's past time for you to make me your wife, so let's do this right now."

Gentle Soul gathered her in his arms. "Everyone prepare for the greatest celebration you have ever had. My woman is finally ready to marry me." Everyone laughed with Gentle Soul. "Dancing Eyes, please bring the bride present I have for Whiskey Woman."

Tempest cried when he presented the horse to her. She was magnificent. "Thank you Husband; I will cherish her always. But, I'm afraid I don't have any gift for you..."

"Oh but you do. Marrying me is the best gift you could give me. I love you Whiskey Woman." He said, as he nuzzled her neck.

Finally, Tempest knew what heaven on earth meant.

About The Author

Kelly Jarrell resides in Eastern Kentucky and this is her second novel. Kelly is a widow, and has two grown Daughter's-Jessica, and Ashley. When Kelly's not writing for a book, she enjoys writing and recording her own songs, which you may find on YouTube under: Kelly aylor jarrell. Kelly can be found on Facebook, under her maiden name: Kelly Aylor. If you would like to buy any of her book's, they are available on Amazon under Kelly Jarrell. If you would like to write Kelly, pls send mail to: Kelly Jarrell, 188 Hidden View Dr. Harold, Ky. 41635

Made in the USA
Lexington, KY
27 November 2016